MOONLIGHT IN VERMONT

Kacy Cross

Based on the Hallmark Channel Original Movie
Teleplay by Michael Nourse and Brian Sawyer & Gregg Rossen
Story by Angela Ruhinda

ISBN: 978-1-947892-13-2

Hallmark
PUBLISHING

www.hallmarkpublishing.com
For more about the movie visit:
www.hallmarkchannel.com/moonlight-in-vermont

TABLE OF CONTENTS

ONE

Spring in Manhattan brought rejuvenation, fresh perspective, and lots of shiny new properties on the market. Fiona Rangely intended to take advantage of all three in her quest to stay on top of the real estate game. Her face graced *Sold!* signs across the city, and as soon as she closed this next deal, she'd beat her own record for the month.

Everyone deserved a place to live that could become a home, where they'd build families and create memories. This conviction had helped Fiona become the queen of Manhattan real estate—that and a better-than-average ability to shut down her emotions during negotiations.

Fiona put on her game face and turned her attention to the only thing standing between her and an unparalleled property with a view of the river.

On a good day, other brokers called Tony Kapucki a shark. It wasn't because he swam really fast. He had a reputation for bleeding every last cent out of a sale and she knew he'd try to take a bite out of this deal too.

He didn't disappoint her.

"Do you realize what's happening in the market?" Tony asked as they squared off over coffee.

"You're dreaming, Tony. You know it's a fair offer." She ignored his nonchalant shrug and leaned in as if about to impart a secret. "And you get to look like a hero presenting it to your client!"

"Fiona." Tony's smirk held a hint of desperation. "I know you."

That meant she had him on the ropes. Now for the final one-two punch. "Then you know to listen to me."

"Eh." Tony's gaze shifted away from hers. "Another few weeks on the market, who knows what my client'll get."

"My guess? Some shaky offers and an angry co-op board. So what's it gonna take to close this deal, and give a nice grandma and her Pekinese a home?"

Throwing in a mention of a dog always helped paint the picture for her opposition, and this was no exception. Tony took the knockout with grace, though he didn't hesitate to tack on a few amendments to the contract that favored his client. No problem. The deal shook out in less than five minutes.

The hustle of the city slapped her with its noise and beautiful chaos the moment Fiona stepped outside the bistro where she'd met Kapucki and handed him his hat. Her client waited for her near the entrance, looking too nervous to sit at one of the sidewalk tables lining the street.

"We've got a deal," Fiona said to the older lady, completely unable to keep her face from splitting into a wide grin. "And you've got a rooftop apartment by the river."

The relief and genuine excitement on her client's face as she processed what had just happened gave Fiona a rush that she couldn't replicate any other way.

"They must have had a hundred offers," the woman gushed as she and Fiona strolled a bit away from the crowd to where they could hear each other. "How'd you do it?"

More like eighty-five offers, to be exact, but who's counting. "Oh, a little creative financing and a whole lot of begging."

"Thank you."

The gratitude in her client's eyes was all the thanks Fiona needed. "Location is everything, and you're gonna love that place."

"Fiona, you're amazing. Let's celebrate." The other woman grasped her arms in genuine enthusiasm, which only made it harder to say no.

Unfortunately, she had to. Nathanial's partners had rented out the poshest watering hole on the Upper East Side, and finally, after eight months of dating, Fiona would be meeting his work colleagues. She'd hoped the first time they were introduced, it would be as Nate's fiancée, but he had yet to take her many hints. The man moved so slowly sometimes!

Maybe she'd drop a few more breadcrumbs. If she

laid a clear path, maybe she'd get a proposal for her birthday, though it was three very long months away.

"Sorry, I can't," Fiona said and threw in, "But congratulations. I'm really happy for you."

Fiona sent her client on her way and palmed her cell phone. It fit into her hand perfectly, almost as if it had been made for her dimensions. This phone saved her life every day. Sometimes she had nightmares about losing it or dropping it onto the tracks at the Franklin Street station near her office in Tribeca. If that happened, she'd be lost, having no contact with the things that comprised her world.

Before she could dial, Nate called. She told him she was on her way. As she looked around for the hired car she'd ordered at the bistro right after Tony caved, she dialed her assistant, Andy, for their hourly check in.

Fiona wasn't a control freak and Andy got that. She might be more of a perfectionist than anything, but really it boiled down to the personal touch. Her clients trusted her with their homes, many of which went for seven-figure price tags. You didn't repay that trust by passing off clients to an assistant. You crossed every *t* and dotted every *i*.

"Andy. Okay, all done for the night?"

Andy cleared his throat. "Small change of plans. The Morrisons' flight tomorrow morning got bumped, so they're leaving on the red eye. Tonight. They need to make a decision before they go to Europe."

That thumping in her ears could *not* be her pulse. It was far too loud.

"But they can't leave town tonight," she returned inanely. *No, no, no.* This was not happening. "I'm showing them the two bedroom tomorrow and the location's amazing, right by their kids' school."

"Sorry, boss. They want you to meet them now," Andy returned matter-of-factly, as if the entire night hadn't just slid into the gutter.

"Now?" she gasped and glanced at her watch. "I just told Nate I would meet him—"

Deep breath. The Morrisons needed a home, a place to raise their children. Nate would understand if she was a teensy bit late. He was special and really cared about her. "You know what, I can do both. See you soon."

Positive thinking had gotten her through more than one sticky situation. It wouldn't fail her now.

When Fiona rushed into the swanky bar hosting Nathanial's work party, her pulse hadn't calmed down since her earlier phone call with Andy. "Late" did not begin to describe her tardiness, but the Morrisons would not be rushed, nor would she have forced them to cut short their tour of the home she'd found for them.

They'd loved the brownstone, and as she'd expected, the location had sealed it for them. Their two kids could walk to the private school they attended, and no less than four restaurants occupied spaces on the corner. The couple had asked Fiona to put in an offer while they were in Europe, so the side trip had been worth it for the commission alone, but knowing she'd given them a home instead of a place to put their stuff—that was why she did what she could to put her clients first.

Nate stood by the bar, looking handsome and devastating in a custom-made suit that fit him so well, her stomach fluttered. The culmination of a perfect evening. She could relax with Nate and tell him about her stellar day. He'd be proud, smiling down at her with his trademark eye twinkle that he reserved just for the lady in his life.

"Nate, I am so sorry!" she called out with an apologetic smile for the man she'd been falling for all these months.

She noted with a bit of trepidation that Nate was the only one in the room. It wasn't *that* late. Barely nine-thirty. Where was everyone else?

When Nate turned to face her, the first inkling that she'd messed up skated through her stomach. There was no trademark twinkle. He did not hug her as he usually did, choosing to stuff his hands in his pants pockets instead. He looked every inch the corporate powerhouse he personified at work...and nothing like the man she wished to spend the rest of the night unwinding with.

"Fiona." The frost in his voice set her back. "Finally."

Scrambling, Fiona shook her head. "My schedule was timed to the minute. But my Uber clipped a food truck and I had to get out and jog the last eight blocks. Listen, I know this was important to you."

Oh, man, was Nate ever annoyed. His lips tightened as he contemplated her. "The partners only meet twice a year."

She knew that, she really did. He'd told her many times how special tonight was. "I'll make it up to you, I promise. My schedule this time of year is just a blitz."

"We're a great couple when we see each other." Nate's face became inaccessible with an expression she'd never seen before. "But I'm not dating your schedule, and lately it seems like you never have time for me."

"So I'll make time—"

"We are who we are. I just think maybe we want different things."

Dumbstruck, she stared at him. That sounded an awful lot like the precursor to a conversation she had not prepared for. He knew how important her career was. Right? And that when you worked in real estate, you had to be at the beck and call of your clients, many of whom worked during the day and required evening showings. Being available and flexible at all times was an integral part of her service.

"Nate, what are you saying?"

"That I'm tired of being just one more ball in your juggling act."

Fiona shook her head automatically, as if that could somehow ward off the awful direction of this conversation.

"Yes, I may be juggling, but I've never *dropped* you." And then it hit her that he wasn't buying. His face had already closed in. "Are you...dropping *me*?"

Her voice broke on the last word and that cued the prick of tears. Unacceptable. Emotions had no place here, and the less he saw how this bombshell was affecting her, the better. She blinked back the tears and stood there without a single way to deflect what she knew was coming.

"I'm just doing what's best for both of us."

His voice was gentle, but it didn't matter. The words pierced through her like bullets. Without another word, she fled the bar and blindly searched for the Uber app on her phone, refusing to cry, refusing to feel. She hated being at the mercy of emotions, especially this sensation as if her chest was about to explode from too much pressure.

This was why she avoided things that made her feel too much. Which meant it was time to lock it down.

That condo near her office with the second bathroom that she'd earmarked for her and Nate—just in case he proposed sooner than she'd expected—had just become the perfect property for one of her clients. First thing in the morning, she'd figure out which one it fit best, ensuring that the demise of her relationship with Nate still had some kind of positive outcome. That was the only way she'd get through this—by focusing on making someone happy through real estate that would become a home.

Two

The next morning, Fiona had enough distance from last night's shocking conclusion that she thought she could tell Angela without breaking down. She'd tried to call Ang at least three times in the long hours before two a.m., when she'd finally fallen into a fitful sleep. But she hadn't been able to dial. Her throat kept closing and she couldn't stand the thought of falling apart, not even with Angela.

Today she needed a sympathetic ear.

Fortunately, her oldest friend answered on the first ring. Calling a therapist during work hours was always dicey and Fiona hated potentially interrupting a session.

Her friend would reschedule a patient for Fiona, no questions asked, but that wasn't necessary for this conversation. It wasn't like the contents of her news would change if she had to wait thirty minutes to hash out the worst thing that had happened to her in recent memory.

"Oh, please tell me you have good news," Angela

begged her. No *hi, how are you?* It was straight to a request that Fiona couldn't fulfill. "I have been listening to sad stories all day long."

Great, so she got to ruin Angela's day too. That was what friends were for, right? "Nate dumped me last night."

"What?" Angela squawked. "Oh, honey."

"I'm just in shock." That was an understatement. No matter how much she tried to spin it, the reality didn't change. Nate hadn't cared enough to give her a second chance, to let her show him that things would be different once her schedule calmed down.

If only the Morrisons' flight hadn't been changed, none of this would have happened. It was pure bad luck, and now she was single. *Again.*

"You know what they say—men are like melons," Angela said. "It's tough to pick a good one."

Fiona pictured Angela sitting on the long leather couch in her office as she talked Fiona through this. That was what Angela did. She made people feel better with nothing more than compassion and a unique, soothing tone in her voice.

Except she was wrong about the situation. For once.

"Nate *is* a good one," Fiona corrected. "And I thought we were destined to be together. I guess destiny fell asleep on the job. Ang, what am I getting wrong? Nate and I had something so special."

Well, no, obviously they didn't or they'd still be together. Clearly the problem lay with Fiona if she couldn't see that her "juggling" act had been making Nate dizzy this whole time.

"Why don't we meet up? There's no problem a good chocolate mousse can't fix."

Angela, bless her, had her back. Thank goodness they'd stuck to each other like glue through everything childhood, high school, and then college had to throw at them, and now this thing called adulthood. Ang had even managed to pull a smile out of Fiona.

"What, did you learn that in advanced psych? No, I would love to but Irwin Lanheim is about to stop by." Irwin was an old friend of Fiona's father—"friend" being relative. They'd been fierce rivals on Wall Street, but now that her dad had moved to Vermont, all of his relationships had changed. Including the one with her. "Who knows, that could be trouble."

"You're you. You can handle anything." Angela didn't stop there. "And Fi? Schedule some time for your feelings."

"I will." She wouldn't. Angela always said stuff like that. It was practically her signature advice. But Fiona wasn't Angela's patient, and feelings didn't get the job done or ease her loneliness. They just got in the way. "I'll talk to you later."

Irwin Lanheim cleared the door of Fiona's office ahead of the receptionist, his broad smile already in place on his handsome jaw. The man did not age and had no less energy despite being closer to retirement age than he liked to admit.

"Fiona," he called with a pleased chuckle as he laid his coat on a side table. "It's been too long."

Fiona rose instantly and met him at the corner of her desk to accept a brief kiss on the cheek, her own smile as big as his. It *had* been too long. "Irwin! I read about the merger. Well done."

He nodded modestly, despite having just successfully led the conglomeration of two of the largest banking enterprises in North America. "Quite the compliment from the toast of New York real estate."

"Sounds better than just being toast," Fiona quipped back, uncomfortable with the praise.

"Yes, it certainly does."

Fiona grinned. Irwin had always appreciated her humor, one of many reasons she liked him the best of her father's old set of friends. "How are the newlyweds?"

Clearing his throat, Irwin put a bit of distance between them and braced both palms on her desk. "Kimberly left me. In fact, the papers were just filed this morning."

Oh, goodness, she'd walked straight into that one. "I am so sorry."

"No," Irwin said graciously. "It is what it is."

Somehow that made it easier to confess her own drama. "We're kind of in the same boat then."

"What, you and Nate?" Irwin's eyebrows came together in concern.

"Nate and I are on a bit of a break," she admitted.

Seemed to be going around. What was wrong with both her and Irwin that they'd picked people to align themselves with who didn't *get* them? Who ran at the first sign of trouble?

"Well, I'm sorry to hear that. Unfortunately, when you work as hard as you and I do, sometimes relationships tend to be a little bit difficult."

And that was why she'd had few qualms about mentioning the blow Nate had dealt her—she and Irwin were cut from the same cloth. She felt a little better knowing that he faced some of the same struggles.

"My parents somehow found a way to make it work, though," she mused, but that just put her back in a contemplative mood about what had gone wrong with Nate. And that wasn't productive.

"Hey." Irwin brightened. "How is your father? He still in Vermont?"

"Yes, he's still running the inn with my stepmom." Amazing how she'd gotten that sentence out and kept a smile plastered across her face. It was a sore spot, and she spent a lot of time trying to forget about the inn that had stolen not only her father from her, but all of her childhood memories. Irwin didn't know that, though.

"What's it been, like five years?" He didn't pause long enough for her to confirm that it had indeed been five very long years since Harris Rangely had pulled up stakes unexpectedly. "I have to say, the city is certainly a lot less fun without my old rival."

It was better that way, actually. Her father had betrayed Fiona's mother's memory by moving away, and now Fiona never had to think about how devastating of a blow it had been. Except when people like Irwin, who'd known her father, brought it up.

"I actually passed our old apartment on the way over," she found herself saying. That was a sore spot too. That apartment had been her *home*, the one she'd shared with her parents, where she'd grown up. "I just can't believe my dad up and left the city like that."

The apartment, where all her greatest moments had happened, belonged to someone else. Vermont had swallowed her father whole, as if the Wall Street tycoon who'd been married to her mother had never existed.

What was *wrong* with her? Nate had done a number on her, for sure, but that was no reason to dump all of her angst on an old friend. "I'm sorry. You did not come here to listen to me reminisce."

"The city is your passion. You take after your mother, and it's that passion that helped you build a great business. But..." Irwin leaned forward, a sure tell that he had gotten to the part where he planned to explain why he'd come by today. "You can do better. In fact, with the merger complete, I want you to run the new real estate arm of my banking interests."

Fiona blinked. As revelations went, that was a doozy. Obviously someone was trying to get her out of the game. Otherwise, why would he assume she was looking for a change? "I'm honored, but my business

19

is great as it is. I'm my own boss. Why would I want to change that?"

"Because you've got a problem," Irwin informed her blithely, hands outstretched as he laid down that provocative statement.

She couldn't not play along, mostly because she had to hear what he'd say next. "Oh, I do?"

"Yeah, there's only one of you. Could you imagine what you might do with a staff of ten? Or a hundred?" He pointed out the window where thousands of properties lay waiting for her special blend of skill and desire to match the right place with the right buyer. "You can craft the Manhattan skyline like it's your own set of Tinkertoys."

Intriguing. Her mind spun off in a hundred directions as she instantly sifted through the possibilities of what this offer entailed. She could build an empire, follow in Barbara Corcoran's footsteps. Maybe even get her own TV show one day. If nothing else, she'd have partners in this business she could trust, who could take some of the load off for when Fiona needed personal time.

Maybe she could even get Nate back. That dangerous thought wouldn't stop swirling through the middle of everything.

Then reality woke her up in a hurry. Commercial real estate had a completely different set of rules, of pitfalls and challenges. Could she do it? Of course. It might even be fun to see if she could dominate that arena as she had residential property. However, it would be a giant increase in responsibility, not to mention adding hours upon hours to her already busy work week.

But what else did she have to do with her time? Nothing. Maybe destiny had handed her this opportunity to make up for the Nate-sized void in her life. Or a potential way to eventually show him that she'd made changes he might appreciate.

Apparently sensing her indecision, Irwin climbed to his feet. "Okay. Just think about it. But not for too long."

As Irwin grabbed his coat to show himself out of her office, Fiona nodded, her mind still whirling with this unexpected decision. Fate had a funny sense of humor. If this had happened two days ago, she'd call Nate immediately to hash out the pros and cons. That was why she'd fallen for him, after all. He had a sharp, strategic mind and he'd always listened to her with this intense focus, then offered his opinion with concise, well-thought-out reasoning.

Well, not anymore. Now she'd make her own decisions based solely on what was good for Fiona Rangely.

Brunch had not been a good decision.

Fiona stared at the exposed brick next to the tiny table Angela had grabbed near the window and reeled back the emotion that seemed to always be so close to the surface these days. The coffee didn't taste right and she couldn't stomach the thought of eating. Normally, she loved people-watching, but every person strolling down the sidewalk outside had a mate. Two by two, they laughed at each other's jokes as they walked, joined at the hip as if they couldn't bear to be separated.

It was nauseating.

Shifting her attention back to Ang, she shook her head. "I shouldn't have come. I'm not brunch-ready yet."

Angela, who had dressed to the nines for the occasion in a gorgeous navy blue sweater set, set down her coffee cup. "Oh, sure you are. You have been working non-stop for, what's it been now, three weeks?"

"Since Nate?" Rhetorical question. Of course that was what she meant. Lately Fiona had categorized everything as Before Nate and After Nate, a practice Angela didn't like. "Oh, twenty-two days and thirteen hours, but I mean, who's counting?"

Ang raised her brows, a sure sign she had a smart-aleck comeback all lined up. "So glad you're not obsessing." But then she rolled her eyes and smoothed back her red curls without mussing her style. "You remind me of this patient I have. Every session, he obsesses about his cat."

Nice. So now Fiona's heartbreak had been lumped into the same category as cat obsessions. "Isn't there something called patient confidentiality?"

"Don't be boring. And don't block your feelings," Ang threw in.

She'd been saying that every chance she had, which Fiona didn't get. It was starting to become annoying, honestly. She had a broken heart here. What else was there to unblock? Did Ang want her to bleed? Cry? What?

"I just can't believe that he dumped me," she mumbled, which wasn't even half of it. "If only I could pay to have my feelings *go away*."

"How do you think I paid for my condo?" Ang said slyly.

If only taking Ang up on her subtle offer to help would work. It wouldn't. Nate hadn't called. Hadn't stopped by. Hadn't given Fiona the slightest indication he even noticed the void in his life where his girlfriend used to be. Maybe he didn't miss her at all, which if true, would be just devastating.

Had she been ignoring his needs *that* much?

If he thought that, maybe he was punishing her for it. Making her feel lonely and abandoned like he'd said he had felt, until he decided she'd had enough and that's when he'd come back. That was kind of mean, if so.

"Never mind," Ang continued, "you know what your problem is? You never slow down long enough for you to actually have feelings."

Fiona's phone vibrated with the special pattern she used for Andy. Perfect time to segue out of this uncomfortable conversation into something that made sense—real estate. "Hold that thought."

Ang pulled the phone from her hand. "My point exactly."

Without the phone as a distraction, memories got the best of her, and this was no exception. "Nate used to love this place. He would get the Reuben on rye. It was his favorite."

"Fiona." Ang's calm voice cut through the scene playing out in her head. The moment Fiona focused on her, she said, "You're going to have to move on."

No. That wasn't happening. She needed to figure this out. There was always a possibility that if she did, Nate would forgive her. They could pick up where they'd left off. There was no law that said she couldn't have hope.

Except Nate had given zero indication that he might be thinking of reconciling.

"Every relationship I'm in just falls apart. What if I'm alone permanently? Really, what if I'm like that half duplex that just sits on the market forever?"

"You need a fresh perspective," Ang told her. "You know, I think we could both use a holiday out of town."

The foreign word rolled around in her head as she tried to put some context around Ang's point. "What, you mean like a *vacation*?"

"Yeah. Let's shake things up a little. Get your mind off of Nate. You can come back here with a fresh start."

Ang's face lit up. "I know just the place. We should go visit your dad. I've always wanted to see the inn."

"The inn?" Now Angela was just talking crazy. Why would Fiona voluntarily visit the place that had supplanted her childhood home? "I don't know. My stepmom is still upset with me for not visiting since last summer. And you know my dad and I have issues." The last time she'd gone up there—which had only happened because Delia harassed her until Fiona took two days off to breeze through—she and her father had barely spoken outside of surface-level chitchat about the inn and its daily functions.

"You need a change of scenery," Ang said firmly and gestured at the bistro's other tables. "Let's face it. Manhattan is ground zero for happy couples. Holding hands through Central Park, shopping along Fifth Avenue, brunch in places like this. I mean... look."

Fiona followed her gesture to spy a couple with their heads together at a nearby table. They weren't even eating, just laughing softly to each other in that way newly-in-love people do when everything is rosy and beautiful.

The couple even had matching scarves. *Gag.*

Angela topped off Exhibit A with, "*That* is my point exactly."

It was an arrow through the gut, all right. The city wasn't a good place to be right now, not if she planned to keep pretending she wasn't devastated.

Then she had a worse thought. She had a much higher chance of running into Nate by haunting the places he liked, which was the real reason brunch had been a bad idea. The breakup had her all turned around.

If nothing else, she needed to be someplace Nate was not. "You sold me. When do we leave?"

THREE

Before she could go all the way to Vermont, Fiona had to clear the air with Delia, her stepmother. When Fiona's father had remarried a couple of years after his wife died, Fiona expected to hate the woman who had replaced her mom. She didn't.

Delia was wonderful, exactly what her lonely dad had needed. She'd never intruded on Fiona's life, had never been anything but supportive and gracious. Her stepmother was everything anyone could hope for: a friend, a confidante, a role model.

Which was why this call had to happen, despite the butterflies in Fiona's stomach. Delia loved her; she knew that. Oddly, their relationship had so many fewer complications than the one Fiona had with her father, which had everything to do with why it was hard to beg forgiveness for not visiting more. It wasn't Delia's fault her husband had moved out to a remote place like Vermont and abandoned everything that was important to Fiona.

But it was Fiona's fault she couldn't get over what she viewed as a betrayal, plain and simple.

Delia answered on the first ring. "Inn at Swan Lake. May I help you?"

Her stepmother sounded so cheerful and so much like unconditional love that this idea started to seem like a good one. She could use a hug from Delia right about now and some supportive, kind words about the horrible thing Nate had done to her. "Hi. It's Fiona."

"Hi, honey! How are you doing?"

Small talk wasn't going to get this apology out any faster. "Listen, before you say anything, I'm sorry it's been so long since I visited."

There was no excuse, so she gave none.

"Oh, honey, that's understandable. I just miss you. Well, we all do," Delia corrected hastily.

Fiona knew her father didn't have a sentimental bone in his body. The Wall Street old guard still talked about his ability to stay calm and unemotional in the face of turmoil. It had been the key to his success...and the whole reason he could dump an apartment full of love and laughter to jet off to Vermont at a moment's notice.

And that was ancient history at this point. Ang needed a vacation. Fiona needed to not run into Nate by accident. Vermont held the key to both. No reason to let her emotions over the past get the best of her. Like father, like daughter.

"Well, that's why I'm calling. Angela and I thought it might be nice to come up tomorrow and see you guys for a few days." She barely got the sentence out before Delia was squealing with happy laughter. "I take it that means you're excited?"

"Yes," Delia said succinctly in case there was still a question.

"We'll just stay four or five days, but only if you have the room."

"Don't be ridiculous, of course we have the room. And your timing couldn't be more perfect. MapleFaire kicks off this weekend."

Fiona smiled just a little. That meant she could shove Angela out the door to sightsee on her own while Fiona nursed her broken heart by lying around in bed all day, phone in hand as she managed a few deals remotely. "Great. See you tomorrow then. Love you. And send my love to Dad."

That was as close as she'd get to being conciliatory toward Harris Rangely.

Fiona looked up to see Irwin strolling into her office. Unannounced. "Irwin. Hi. I wasn't expecting to see you."

Did they have an appointment she'd forgotten about? No way. Unless she needed this vacation even more than Angela insisted she did.

"And I wasn't expecting to have to chase you down," Irwin said.

Oh. This was about the job offer that she'd been sitting on for goodness knows what reason. "I'm sorry. I really have to apologize—"

"Am I detecting a bit of hesitation?"

"No." *Yes.* But she couldn't let him know that her head hadn't been in the game since Nate had dumped her. Scrambling, she gave him the best excuse she could think of. "I'm just going up to visit my dad in Vermont, and—"

"This is an offer of a lifetime," Irwin reminded her, and it unsettled her stomach that he felt he needed to. "You'll be the queen of New York real estate. What more could you want?"

Good question. The offer was amazing. It was Fiona that was the problem. She couldn't stop wondering if this job might be one more thing standing in the way of finding the man she'd always envisioned making her happy.

Out of the frying pan, into the fire?

She'd never know if she didn't jump. But giving up her solo practice was a huge step.

"Just a few more days to clear my head," she begged.

Good. The request was vague enough that she wasn't committing, but neither was she saying no. Maybe she *did* need this vacation. Perfect opportunity to get herself over this weird hump. She was going to take the job. It was indeed a once in a lifetime opportunity, and she hadn't found the right man without it, had she?

"All right," Irwin said kindly. "Give your father my best."

"I will."

"We'll talk soon." Irwin posed it like a statement not a question and Fiona appreciated the grace.

"Absolutely." She was already formulating her acceptance, which she'd give him after letting Ang drag her to Vermont. Irwin deserved a one hundred percent whole-hearted commitment and nothing less.

Spring in Vermont apparently meant something different than it did in New York. Instead of delicate budding flowers and cute yellow ducks, Vermont got snow. Lots and lots of snow.

If Fiona didn't know better, she'd think they'd gone back in time, and not just a few months. Decades. Everything here had that old-world feel to it, the same kind she sometimes got when crossing the threshold of a building on the Lower East Side that hadn't changed since the early part of last century. Ghosts of days gone by flitted through the very atmosphere, weighing everything down with a sense of permanence and roots.

That part, she appreciated.

"It is so pretty here," Angela gushed as Fiona drove past yet another white field that looked exactly like the adjacent white field. "Fun fact. Did you know Vermont has more cows per capita than any other state?"

"And it snows in the springtime," Fiona couldn't help but add as they passed another field covered in white flakes. *Come on.* Some variety would be nice right about now. "Can you check my phone and see if I have service yet, please?"

"What?" Ang sputtered. "No. No more work."

Ang should know by now that Fiona's real estate brain didn't just shut off because her friend had willed it to be so. "Just because I'm out of town doesn't mean my clients have to know that."

"Okay, you have to let it go. You are here to relax and enjoy." Ang punctuated each word with a smooth hand slicing through the air.

"And forget," she muttered. Easier said than done. "I'm nervous about seeing my dad."

Work provided a great distraction. Without it, emotions threatened to take over.

If anyone would get that, Ang would, though Fiona hadn't meant to blurt it out like she expected free therapy. There was a fine line when you had a psychologist for a best friend.

"Five whole days of heartfelt healing ahead," Ang spouted enthusiastically, which Fiona had totally asked for by opening her big mouth.

If it was that easy to heal the rift with her dad, she would have done it already. She hated that they were at odds. Hated it. It was rough on Delia and even sometimes got in the way of Fiona's relationship with her brother, Brandon.

Of course, having a good relationship with Delia meant that her stepmom sometimes came on a little strong when expressing her concern for Fiona and her life.

"And some heartfelt grilling from my stepmom about why Nate and I broke up." *Yay*. Delia meant well. It was just a lot harder to maintain the façade with someone who wouldn't hesitate to ask probing questions, like what Fiona had done to mend things. "And we're here."

A sign with a black swan at the top and The Inn at Swan Lake across the bottom marked the way. Fiona drove the rental crossover SUV up the lane past a picturesque barn like the kind in storybooks with the large white X over the door and shuttered haylofts. The house nestled into the apex of the road where it circled back to the main highway. Horses grazed nearby, peacefully chomping on whatever horses ate when their food source had been buried by a layer of snow.

Throwing the car in park directly in front of the house that doubled as the inn, Fiona stepped out, the chill in the air stealing her breath for a moment. "Welcome to paradise. Or Siberia. This is definitely the frozen tundra."

"This is adorable," Ang said, her head swiveling around to take it all in so fast that it was a wonder she registered anything. "I love it."

"Sure, Vermont is beautiful," Fiona allowed and flung a hand at the charming two story house with a generously wide wraparound porch. "This only cost me my childhood home."

"Oh, you poor thing." There came Ang's sarcasm,

which meant Fiona had blathered on about it too long, apparently.

Can't have it both ways, Ang. If she wanted Fiona to express her feelings about things, then she was going to have to hear about it too, now wasn't she?

A racket on the other side of the car cut her off before she could remind Ang that she'd been the one to insist Fiona get in touch with her inner crybaby. Turning simultaneously, both women got an eyeful of the best scenery in Vermont thus far—about a hundred yards away, a rugged, clean-cut guy loaded wood into a wheelbarrow.

Hello. He bent to pick up another log and Fiona couldn't help but notice how he moved, as if comfortable in his own skin. Very nice. Hey, she might be nursing a broken heart, but there was absolutely nothing broken about her eyes.

"Who is that?" Fiona murmured. "A groundskeeper or something?"

"I don't know." Ang waggled her brows. "He's cute, though."

Yes, he was. Straight out of an LLBean catalogue, and apparently he lifted weights, too, because some of those logs were not small. This was the kind of scenery Fiona could really appreciate.

Angela's cell phone rang. "Oh, I have service. What part of 'I'm on vacation' did you not understand?" she bit out to whoever had called as she paced away.

So not fair that Ang had reception and Fiona didn't. It was one more cruel joke in a long line of disappointments this Spring. "Oh, this is definitely not Manhattan."

Only the sky heard her because this place put new meaning in the term "remote." Even the cute groundskeeper couldn't hold her attention. A rooster crowed and as she glanced toward it, a huge pile of mushrooms near her feet caught her attention. They were growing right there on a pile of logs near the drive.

"Gross." She kicked at them but there were a lot and they held on tenaciously. Some of the slimy roots stuck to her Fendi boots that she'd snagged at an end-of-season sale at Barney's only two weeks ago. "Yuck."

"Hey, whoa!" The cute groundskeeper rushed her suddenly, peeling off his gloves as he crossed to the pile of logs she'd been kicking, his expression incredulous. "What are you *doing*?"

"I'm just getting rid of these mushrooms." Not that she had to explain herself to him. "Eyesores like that can really decrease a property's value."

Everyone knew that. And they were the first thing guests would see as they pulled up in the circular drive. Delia and her father clearly needed someone with her skills to walk the property line in search of these scenarios.

His gaze lit on the crushed mushrooms and his expression fell. There was no question that she'd rained on his parade somehow. As if she'd kicked a puppy instead of fungus, he bent down and gathered the bunch into his hands protectively.

35

"These are not just mushrooms." He towered over her as he spread his hands open to show her. "They're *oyster* mushrooms."

"Ohhhh-kay. Oyster mushrooms," Fiona repeated since the distinction clearly meant something to him. Wow, he was really tall. She had to crane her neck to look up at him. "Sorry."

"They're really delicious and extremely rare for this early in the season," he informed her in a tender voice better reserved for when speaking of a dearly departed relative.

Wait, delicious? As in he'd planned to *eat* them? Food came wrapped in plastic at the grocery store, not clinging to a log *outside*. In the elements. Where bugs and stuff could crawl on it.

"Well, I didn't mean to interrupt your harvest," she shot back.

He might be cute but he had this way of smirking that put her back up, as if she were a bumbling idiot from the city who couldn't possibly know the secrets of Vermont real estate, particularly when it came to property value.

"I still gotta take mushroom soup off the menu," he informed her, his breath turning white in the chilly air as he turned his back on her.

"Menu." The word did not compute. "Menu for what?"

But the not-so-cute-after-all groundskeeper had already walked away, clearly not interested in continuing a conversation with Fiona the Destroyer.

The guy might have cheekbones to spare, but he'd left his personality in bed this morning. Until he found it, she'd be happy to stay indoors, well away from the surly groundskeeper.

"Fi!" a male voice behind her called out and she whirled.

The only male she cared about at this moment charged down the steps and rounded the car, his smile wide and welcoming.

"Brandon!"

Before she could blink, her brother engulfed her in a hug and everything bad that had happened thus far melted away. It had been far too long since she'd seen him, a by-product of the feud with her father since Brandon had been living here at the inn for two or three years now. The former tech-exec couldn't seem to find his footing in the city, so he'd exited stage left for Vermont, which meant he and Fiona didn't get to have dinner on a regular basis anymore.

Shame. She might have to bend a little more about visiting or she'd keep missing her brother. Delia too, for that matter.

"Hi, Brandon," Angela called in a singsong voice she reserved for Fiona's brother.

He stiffened slightly and pulled away from Fiona, turning to greet the redhead whom he'd long considered the bane of his existence. "Angela."

His tone changed when he talked to Fiona's childhood friend, as well. If the two of them couldn't see that the reason they were always so weird with each other was because they belonged together, then she wasn't going to tell them. They had to figure it out on their own.

"The trouble twins return," he announced as he glanced back and forth between the two of them, though Fiona didn't miss that his gaze lingered on Ang.

"Awww." Angela punched him on the arm the way a woman does when she wants to touch a man without cluing him in that she liked him. "You still sore about those snow cones?"

"The snow cones that ended up on my head?"

They'd totally edged out Fiona, facing each other as if there was no one else in the world, which amused her. The air fairly crackled between them.

Ang slid a finger through her hair to tuck it behind her ear as she gave Brandon a saucy smile. "From how I recall it, I was ten and you pulled my hair first."

Brandon scoffed and said something else that Fiona didn't catch because Surly Groundskeeper had lifted the wheelbarrow and pushed it toward the back of the house. There was no denying that watching that man leave had definite appeal—she got the best view of him and she couldn't see that annoying smirk on his face.

"Fiona," Angela snapped in a way that indicated it wasn't the first time she'd said her name. "Back me up on this."

"Oh no." Fiona shook her head and focused on her brother. "I'm not getting in the middle of it. I can't believe you're still living here."

Brandon jumped on the subject change. "It's only temporary. Just like it was last summer."

"And the summer before that and the summer before that," Fiona finished with an indulgent eye roll. He'd had a run of bad luck with his dotcom business in New York. She couldn't blame him for taking time to clear his head.

She'd come to Vermont for the same reason, after all.

"I know. But you know what? I won't knock it. Helping Dad keep this place running is a better workout that I ever got in any gym. Although I do miss being in the center of things."

Of course he did. What sane person would pick Vermont over New York on a permanent basis? Only one with a strong sense of family, which he had in spades. "I'm sure your tech-wizard side will rise again."

"I hope you're right," Brandon admitted, which told Fiona he wasn't as happy here as he pretended. "You guys go on inside and I'll grab your bags."

Fiona nodded and climbed the stairs to the wide wrap-around porch. Trailing her, Ang leaned in and murmured, "He's working out now?"

They barely made it across the threshold before a blonde dynamo nearly bowled them over. "Fiona!"

Her stepmother, Delia, swept her up in a hug. The last year of being apart vanished and Fiona settled into her stepmother's embrace with ease as if they'd just seen each other yesterday. Delia had that way about her. No one stayed a stranger, friends only got closer and family—that was forever. Fiona didn't even mind the slight gleam of concern in Delia's eyes that meant she would definitely be circling back to the breakup with Nate soon. Very soon.

Maybe telling Delia about it would be the final step Fiona needed to let it go. If nothing else happened on this trip than that, it would be time well spent.

Turning her attention to Ang, Delia hugged her as well, murmuring hellos and welcomes with a broad smile.

"Oh, my gosh, it's been so long since I've seen you," Delia exclaimed.

"I know," Fiona cut in quickly. "It's only been since last summer, though."

That excuse didn't assuage her guilt. Delia loved her and wanted to spend time with her. It was that simple, and Delia didn't understand why Fiona couldn't put aside the difficulties with her father. No one did. Fiona included. Her father refused to talk about his reasons for selling the apartment that Fiona had loved, and therefore, Fiona refused to forgive him.

"When you run an inn, that's two hundred bookings ago, so for me, it feels like forever," Delia said with a smile. "I'm just so glad you're home."

Ugh. Fiona's insides curled up at the term. "Do we have to call it home?"

This was not her home. The apartment overlooking the park where she'd lived with her mother and father—*that* got the label "home," and nothing Delia or her father could do or say would change that. If only one of them understood how lost and adrift she'd felt after learning it had been sold…

But she couldn't dwell on that or she'd cave in to the emotions that she'd rather die than admit to.

"Yes. You and your father are going to leave this little tiff behind you on this trip," Delia informed her in that no-nonsense voice that brooked no arguments. "Okay?"

"Okay," Fiona agreed, mostly because she knew it was what Delia wanted to hear. And also because it wasn't really a question. It was a strongly encouraged suggestion, and Fiona hated causing Delia strife in the first place. She wanted it to be true, too, so she'd fake it until it was, if for no other reason than to make Delia happy.

A familiar voice rang out from the hall behind them. "Towels are out of the dryer and need to be folded before the new check-ins arrive."

Fiona's father came into view carrying a laundry basket. *A laundry basket.*

"Some of the new check-ins are already here," Fiona informed her father with a laugh designed to cover that she was really glad to see him, difficulties aside.

Harris immediately dropped his basket and pulled Fiona into a hug before she could protest, and then all she could do was hang on. Her father loved her. He didn't have to say it all the time for it to be true. She could feel it in his embrace. That was enough for now.

She could put aside her feelings. No problem. Just like she'd been doing for years.

"Welcome home," he said enthusiastically, then caught Delia's chopping motion at her neck and amended quickly to, "Welcome here. So... How's life in the Big Apple?"

"Great. This might refresh your memory." Thrilled at the chance to segue off difficult subjects, Fiona rifled through her bag and pulled out Delia's gift wrapped in crackly gold paper tied with curly-q ribbons. "Brought you a bottle of your favorite perfume from 5th Avenue."

"You didn't have to do that," Delia protested but the delight in her eyes told a different story. "Thank you."

"Oh, it's nothing." Delia had filled so many gaps in Fiona's life that the gift couldn't begin to hold all of her gratitude.

Ang handed Harris a bag. "Oh, and here are some real bagels from Zabar's."

That was the real hit. Harris's eyes rounded and he took the bag so carefully, Fiona double-checked to be sure Ang hadn't handed him a live baby.

"Oh, man! Thank you both." Something beyond Angela's shoulder caught Harris's attention and he jerked his chin in that direction, bagels all but forgotten. "There he is. Fiona, this is Derek. He studied in Paris. He's a culinary genius. The inn's pride and joy."

The world clicked into slow motion as the

42

Mushroom Man from outside strode through the dining area off the reception hall. *Of course.* She muttered to Angela, "Oh, the wise-guy groundskeeper?"

Genius, huh? That remained to be seen. At least that answered her *What menu?* question.

Brandon joined the party, throwing in his own two cents on the matter. "He's our new head chef and fingers crossed, soon to be the first Michelin star chef in Vermont."

Derek sauntered over, smirk firmly in place across his chiseled jaw. "Oh, I believe we've met before. And mushroom soup is *still* off the menu."

"The guy's very particular about his mushrooms," Fiona said to her father with an eye roll that she couldn't quite help.

"Yeah," Harris returned with a quizzical expression as if Fiona had told a joke with a punchline he didn't quite get. "And a true artist who needs to focus."

Derek nodded once and carried off a basket of rolls. Wow, was he ever anti-social.

"I've persuaded some of the top restaurant bloggers in New England to come later this week, so he needs to be in prime form." Harris waggled his hand. "Bookings have been down a little bit and we could use the press."

Oh no. Now Fiona felt terrible for giving Derek a hard time about the mushrooms. Clearly her father and Delia were depending on this new head chef to help pick up their business. Well, Derek could have been a little less confrontational about how she'd accidentally messed up his precious menu.

Harris continued. "Tomorrow we have more guests arriving and thanks to Brandon, we've updated our website. We've started to market to the hip millennial crowd."

Delia nodded enthusiastically but Fiona had to laugh. "Hip *millennial* crowd? That just does not sound right coming out of your mouth, Dad."

"Which reminds me…" Brandon trailed off as he held up his phone and wandered off to go do some mysterious inn task. Harris followed him, clearly on a similar mission, leaving Delia beaming at Fiona and Ang.

"Let's get you settled!" she said and tucked Fiona's hand in her capable one. "You can relax and enjoy yourself. And then later on, you can tell me all about your breakup with Nate."

So close. For a minute there, Fiona had thought the subject wasn't going to come up. Hopefully her smile didn't look as pained as it felt, but Delia had vanished already.

"Yay, can't wait!" she said to Ang, her voice dripping with irony. And so she had her marching orders from everyone else. Get over Nate. Get over the tiff with her father. Relax. No work.

When would someone ask Fiona what *she* wanted to do?

FOUR

ock-a-doodle-doo.

C   The cry sounded again, just outside Fiona's window. Groaning, she half lifted her head, saw it was the crack-of-dawn-thirty and slammed the pillow down over her ears.

Didn't help. The crowing continued until it was ridiculous.

If anyone *did* bother to ask Fiona what she wanted to do, item number one on her list had just become throttle that rooster. Shoving the pillow aside, Fiona sat up.

"I'm trapped in Farmville," she muttered and palmed her phone, not that she had any hope it would magically have gained a signal. She'd done everything she could think of last night in an attempt to connect, but no. Cell phone towers didn't seem to exist here.

Something loud and un-rooster-like cut through the air outside her window. *Thwack.* City noise, Fiona could handle, would welcome. That had purpose and value. This thwacking noise? No. Just no.

She let the phone drop to the nightstand and flung the sheets back so she could roll out of bed to address the racket. Mushroom Man stood nearly even with her window chopping wood. *Chopping wood* as if people weren't trying to sleep around here.

The window opened with one of those old-fashioned rollers. Fiona wheeled the handle in a circle until the window yawned wide enough for her to call through it. "Um, are you aware it's not even six a.m.?"

Derek scarcely bothered to glance over his shoulder. "Well then, I'm late. This should have been done by five-thirty."

He immediately turned back to his log splitting routine and cleaved through another one. It halved neatly and Fiona grudgingly noted that he'd barely put much effort into it at all. He was cute, dang it, even when he was being ornery.

It put Fiona's back up. "Isn't it a little early for all this racket?"

"If I don't get this birch cut, there'll be no smoked salmon for dinner." And then he muttered, "New York princess," under his breath but loudly enough that she heard him anyway, which had likely been his intent.

"Vermont lumberjack," she returned cattily and rolled her window shut.

Since she was up, there was no excuse not to take a run, though surely there was far less to see on her route here than there was in the city. She'd have to make the best of it. But first, breakfast. That would put her in a more positive frame of mind.

Vermont was not going to break her.

Morning had long been Derek Price's favorite time of day. He'd taken to getting up early in Paris, before the city fully woke for the day. He'd had a top floor apartment in the 10th arrondissement, tiny but serviceable, and the window opened up with a view over the rooftops.

The day hadn't started yet, so the sun would just peek over the tops of the buildings, lighting on the spires of Sacre-Coeur, the white basilica on the hill. It was like a sign. That was when Derek knew he'd made the right choice to become a chef.

It hadn't always been an easy road. But once he'd landed this dream job at Inn at Swan Lake, his life finally clicked onto the right track. He'd carved out a place here where he could build something meaningful. Put down roots in the Vermont soil where he belonged. He liked stability, traditions and people who said what they meant, in that order.

Which meant that interlopers in his kitchen were not necessarily welcome, particularly in the form of one Fiona Rangely, who had decided to become the thorn in his side, apparently.

She came into the room wearing an explosion of purple fitness wear, her long brown hair caught back in a shiny ponytail. With running shoes on her feet, no one could mistake the New York princess's aim to go for a jog this morning. In the snow. Where there was ice.

Derek shook his head and laid down the knife he'd been using to pare pineapple for the fruit sauce he planned to drizzle over the wood-smoked salmon he'd mentioned to Fiona

"Can I help you?" he called out as he met her in front of the pantry she'd been about to open.

Fiona whirled, clearly startled, though why she'd expected the place to be empty when he had guests to feed remained a mystery to him.

"Oh, no thank you," she said sweetly. "You were already helpful enough with the wakeup call."

That was more Harris's daughter's speed—acerbic wit slathered in charm. He shouldn't encourage it so much, but he just wanted to see what came out of her mouth next.

Which is why when she reached for the pantry door again, he closed it firmly. "My kitchen. So what can I get for you?"

Fiona sighed and then smiled in that way Derek didn't trust for an instant.

"We got off to a rocky start," she said. "But why don't you just do your thing? I'm going to grab some food and go for a run."

And then she actually tried to open the pantry door again. Man, the message was not getting through here and he had dinner prep to do, which took all day. Derek closed it with a click, which put him much closer to Fiona. She smelled…expensive. Nice. But definitely higher maintenance than he typically liked.

"Again. My kitchen."

They stared at each other for a long beat, and it was a moment laden with more things than Derek could sort. Surprising things. Not just two strong-willed people facing off, but a spark.

Huh. Hadn't seen that one coming. Sure, Fiona was attractive in a non-subjective way, same as a sunset was beautiful. But she had that attitude. Well, maybe he kind of liked that too.

"Fine," she said and it was clearly not fine, but it broke the odd tension. She handed him a folded piece of paper. "Have it your way. Gluten-free, no soy, no dairy diet."

He scarcely glanced at the list because…come on. "Food allergies."

It wasn't a question. Only someone who had no choice would deliberately go gluten-free, soy-free and dairy-free. Might as well add cardboard and sawdust to the list.

"No, my nutritionist has this amazing—"

Decisively, Derek ripped the list in half and threw it on the counter. If he never heard about it again, it would be too soon.

"What are you doing?" Fiona squeaked and picked up the pieces, trying to fit them back together. He should have thrown it in the fireplace.

"Don't worry," he advised her. "I've got breakfast covered. You're going to love it."

Because it had food in it. The kind that took hours to make, which meant it was worth it. He poured her a cup of coffee from the French press on the counter and handed it to her as he fetched a plate from the cupboard.

"Maybe I don't drink coffee," Fiona said primly as she accepted the cup with hungry eyes that had already devoured the first sip.

"You? Please." She had *caffeine addict* written all over her. She'd need it to speed through her day as she missed all the greatness of Vermont around her because she was too much in a hurry to appreciate the small things.

Pulling a pan from the oven with a dishtowel, he put fresh cinnamon rolls on the counter and just caught her sipping the coffee from the corner of his eye, a note of bliss on her face that he could get used to seeing a whole lot more.

When people enjoyed something he'd made, that was the best. It was why he'd become a chef—to feed people good food that nourished them body and spirit.

She watched him pull a roll off the tray and as he put it on a plate, she waved at the pan. "Just so you know, I'm on a carb free diet."

"Until now." Wow, she really needed to loosen up. Like a lot. She treated food as a punishment of some sort, skipping all the good things about eating, particularly the enjoyment part.

Her gaze never shifted from the roll in his hand though, no matter how much she protested. Just to prove the point, he took extra time with the glaze, coating the roll twice with his brush.

"Literally watching paint dry here," she said, revealing more than she'd probably intended, like how much she wanted this roll.

"Just give me a second," he told her with a smile. She clearly needed to learn the art of patience. All good things happened when you took the time to do it right.

She sighed and palmed her phone, tapping at the screen since apparently she couldn't just stand there and drink the fantastic coffee he'd made for her. "My cell gets really bad reception here. Do you know where I can get better service?"

"The world can't function for a day without your input?" He glanced up at her as he finished off the glaze.

"That wasn't the question."

"Try outside. A high place, a hill, a barn. Horse." He handed her the roll and she took it without protest.

"Thank you. So helpful."

He had to grin. Her mouth was something else. He liked watching her eat his cinnamon rolls. She took a small bite the way a kid does when he isn't sure he wants what his mother put in front of him, testing it out before fully committing.

"Well?" he couldn't help but ask. He wanted her to like what he cooked. Otherwise there was no point in doing it.

"It's not terrible," she allowed graciously.

That was likely the highest praise he would get. But she did like it, he could tell. The bliss stealing over her features was a dead giveaway. With a knowing smile, he turned to close the oven. While he was distracted, she chose that moment to really bite into it in the way a roll of that stature was meant to be eaten.

He let her have her fun and pretended to be occupied so she could enjoy in peace, but when he turned around a few beats later, she'd vanished. There was a telltale hole in the pan of rolls where she'd snagged a second one, though.

"Not terrible," he repeated to the empty kitchen and that put a smile on his face he wouldn't be able to wipe off for some time.

Hurricane Fiona had blown through his kitchen and he had a feeling she'd rain on his menus a few more times before she went back to New York.

Fiona ran until she thought she might have worked off a quarter of one of Derek's amazing sticky-sweet cinnamon rolls, then ran more to try for another quarter. Running in Vermont was nothing like running in New York. It was all the same: white, white, more white, oh look a tree, more white.

And no amount of running had worked off the distinct *awareness* she'd had of Derek back there in the kitchen. What was that? She didn't even like him.

Okay, he was good-looking with those New England cheekbones and long lean body that didn't suck to watch when he moved. But other than that, he had cocky smugness down to a science. An answer for everything. Little respect for healthy eating.

But he did have charm to spare and, holy cow, could that man bake.

Pausing to catch her breath—and no, she was not stopping to examine whether Derek had something to do with why she was out of breath either—she put a hand on a blue tractor that was parked outside of a dilapidated old barn. The tractor didn't seem to be much newer or in any better condition. When she looked into the adjacent field, an equally old man stood just inside the gate with a bale of hay. Grizzled and at one with the land, he wore plaid like it had been invented for him and a fierce scowl on his face.

Fiona waved. "Hello."

The man paused long enough to acknowledge that someone had spoken to him but the look he gave her held no warmth at all. And then he turned back to his task without uttering a word.

"Good morning to you too," she muttered and held up her cell phone in search of those elusive bars. "Come on, signal… signal… Oooh, signal!"

The screen lit up with text messages and missed calls, which she ignored in favor of dialing. When Andy answered, she spilled a litany of instructions at the poor man in fear of not getting something out before she lost the signal. Which is what happened.

In the middle of her spiel. With a sad beep, the phone died, cutting her off mid-stream.

"Andy!" No Andy.

So much for that. She pocketed the phone and ran back to the inn. In the latest in a long string of unfortunately-timed meetings, Derek came out of the house right when she got there.

"Hey," he called as if he was actually happy to see her, which was a nice change from the chilly non-greeting she'd just gotten up the road. "Help me out a second. I'm late on brunch."

He handed her a basket lined with a dishtowel and that was so intriguing, she followed him. And then she caught sight of the brown and red bird standing on a hay bale outside the house. That looked suspiciously like the other half of her wakeup call.

"Is this where that rooster lives?" She pointed at the offending bird. "'Cause he and I are having a talk."

"Yeah, I named him Swatch," Derek said easily. "He thinks he's a clock."

This was almost a pleasant conversation. She could stand a bit more of nice Derek. "Do you think he knows how to get a cell phone signal? This is Vermont, not Timbuktu."

Derek led her into a greenhouse full of vibrant plants that shouldn't be thriving with snow still on the ground. But the explosion of green told a different story. Clearly someone took very good care of the plants in here. Derek, unless she missed her guess. He had that no-one-touches-my-stuff vibe about him, all right.

"The signal is pretty sketchy up here." He turned his attention to a small-leafed plant in the corner, but then glanced slyly over his shoulder. "Anyway, aren't you supposed to be relaxing after that breakup of yours?"

The squeak that came out of Fiona's mouth wasn't entirely human. So much for civil conversation. He could have gone all day without mentioning that, and how had he heard that anyway? Surely Delia hadn't—

"The staff gossips." Derek cut some of the small leaves from the plant and put them in her basket. "Probably wise that you learn that now."

Well, someone had overheard her talking to Delia then and should definitely be fired, whoever it was. "It's no wonder. There's absolutely nothing to do up here."

Derek scoffed. "There's plenty to do up here."

"Oh really, like what? Growing your own herbs? Because that looks really entertaining."

What was it about this man? He got under her skin like nobody's business. She was never this catty with Nate. Of course, Nate did nothing to elicit such a response. All Derek had to do was stand there and all of these things welled up from inside her...

"Exactly," he said as if he hadn't noticed her sarcasm. "Everything I serve is locally sourced. And what I can't grow, I buy from local farms. Mostly."

He rubbed some of the plant leaves between his

fingers and held them out for her to inhale. Smelled like fresh herbs to her, not that she had any hope of identifying the slightly spicy scent.

Then she made the mistake of glancing up. And immediately fell into Derek's enigmatic silvery gaze. It bored through her, tripping her pulse as they stared at each other, and she did not like how easily he affected her. How easily it seemed like he saw right through her into the inside parts that no one had access to.

"Mostly?" she prodded, but only to distract herself from the unsettling way Derek was looking at her.

"Sometimes I can't get the fresh vegetables I really need. But I'm working on a solution."

In spite of herself, she was curious. "What's that?"

"The neighbor is selling off one of the fields on his farm. The fellow up the road."

"Oh, yeah, the kind of cranky guy who favors plaid." He'd looked at her so strangely, as if he didn't like her, which made no sense when they'd never met. And she was a very nice person. Most of the time. Present company excluded maybe, but only because she couldn't help herself.

"That's him. Only problem is old Chauncey refuses to sell to me."

Fiona rolled her eyes. "I'm shocked that you would rub someone the wrong way."

"Thank you," he shot back with one of his smart-aleck grins. "I have a brunch to prepare."

With that, he left the greenhouse, leaving Fiona with nothing to do but follow him through the door, wondering how on earth she'd exited a run-in with Derek and still had all her skin.

That man was something else. He gave as good as he got and didn't get offended when her sarcasm gene went a little haywire. Somehow, she'd started to like him a tiny bit.

And she'd take *that* to her grave, thank you very much.

FIVE

As Fiona wandered toward the house, she spied her dad in the cute gray barn with white trim. So amused by the idea of her father pulling hay bales out of the loft, she ducked inside. Bonus—she wouldn't accidentally run into Derek at the house. One run-in per hour was more than enough.

Her father dropped a bale to the solid wood floor below the loft. It hit with a thud, raising a cloud of dust.

Fiona smiled up at him, hands on her hips. "If your old pals on Wall Street could see you now…"

Chuckling, Harris strode down the stairs with his usual vigor. "Look around. This place holds more value to me than any portfolio ever could. I could not be happier. I think maybe you could be happy here someday too. You think that's possible?"

And that was the problem. The whole reason she and her dad were at odds. He still couldn't seem to understand that her heart was in New York, not here with all the livestock and *locally-sourced food*.

Once they'd been on the same wavelength. Before her mom had died. Was that the only thing that truly tied them together? Now that her mother wasn't here to keep the peace, were she and her father destined to be strangers?

"Dad." She stared at her feet for a second as she pushed back the tightness in her throat. "I would have been happy with our old place by the park. But we both know that ship has sailed."

Her father kicked the hay bale until it was butt up against another one. "Why do you always have to bring up the past?"

Because if she didn't, who would? Who would be the keeper of memories, particularly those of her mom, since the building where they'd lived wasn't accessible anymore? Memories lived in the boards underfoot, in the walls surrounding you. In the ceiling that had seen years of laughter and tears.

"Why do you always want to forget it?" she countered. "I mean, I know you deserved a fresh start, but that was my history too. It would have been nice to know you were selling."

Instead, she'd been blindsided by the casual phone call, as if her entire life hadn't just upended in one minute.

"You were in college," her father protested. "Besides it had to be done."

Yeah, she'd heard that one before. Many times. It was his old fallback excuse, as if a college student couldn't understand real life decisions or offer any bit of advice. To at least have been consulted... But no. This wound still festered, all these years later.

"Look, I got a million things I gotta do," Harris said as he rolled a hay bale toward one of the horse stalls. "We've got a beautiful weekend shaping up. Brandon's online promotions are starting to pay off."

Nothing ever changed. When Fiona wanted to lay it all out there, her father changed the subject, usually to reiterate how busy he was. No time for emotions. That was the Rangely way.

Fiona sighed. So much for heartfelt healing over the next few days. "Let's get some coffee."

Her dad slung an arm around her and walked with her back to the house like nothing was wrong. He did denial better than anyone on the planet. And the voices in her head could shut up anytime about how far that apple fell from the tree, which was not far at all.

"There's a French press in the kitchen," he said as they cleared the front door of the main house. And then she lost him to the new guests who were standing in the foyer looking around expectantly. A couple. Young, urban, clearly lovers. *Ugh.*

"You made it!" Harris exclaimed and tapped the guest registration book. "I heard about the mess on the Mass Pike. I gotcha right here."

Fiona left him to his inn owner speech and wandered through the great room. Another couple sat near the fire rubbing noses like teenagers and clinking champagne glasses full of orange juice. More love in the air.

Mercifully, she spied Ang at the table in the breakfast area wolfing down food like she'd never eaten before. "There you are. You could sleep through an explosion."

"Not an explosion of flavor." She pointed to her plate. "Fi, this omelet is amazing. The chef here is a genius."

"He certainly thinks so." And that made her feel petty. It wasn't his fault this inn suddenly had forty-seven reminders of her singlehood being shoved down her throat. She slid into the vacant seat at Ang's side. "Listen, we've got to get out of here. This place is infested."

Ang dropped her fork and backed away from the omelet. "With what?"

"With couples." Duh. Did Ang even *glance* around while she worshipped Derek's omelet? "We left the Big Apple and ended up in Mayberry. Look around you. We've got lovebirds over here dressed for hiking, Mustache Mike over there with blondie is checking in, and this happy couple over here is probably celebrating the first time they kissed. Where is the subway noise when I need it?"

As she'd pointed out each couple, Ang followed the covert hand gestures with a fair amount of amusement. "Honey, we just got here."

"And we can be home by dinner," Fiona threw in brightly.

"No, there's lots of great stuff for us to do here. You need to open yourself up to new experiences." Ang picked up a brochure by her plate and held it up. "I've got one word for you. MapleFaire."

Fiona didn't miss her enthusiasm. This was important to Ang, and Fiona's broken heart had reared its ugly head at the most inconvenient time. "Yeah. I've heard about it. Some local ritual involving trees. I've managed to avoid it all these years."

On purpose. There was no mistaking the "fun is therapy" in Ang's tone either. She thought it would be good for Fiona, which made it even less appealing in light of all the other stuff Ang had insisted would happen on this trip—like making up with her father.

"No, look." She opened the brochure to read from it. "Five days of rustic festivities around town. This sounds super fun. And it starts today."

"Fine. Whatever. Just anywhere but here."

The Teenaged Kisses couple were at it again. Didn't they know people could see them? Hear them giggling to each other?

Ang forked up a bite of omelet. "You have got to try this."

The only thing Fiona had to do was go to her room and bury her head in the sand. This morning hadn't started off very well. It could only go downhill from here.

The heart of MapleFaire teemed with activity and Angela Walker loved every second of it. She'd become a psychologist because she genuinely loved people. They fascinated her, and there was no better place on earth to study them than at the intersection of entertainment and tradition.

MapleFaire had deep roots in the community and everyone here had a story. She wished she could hear them all. Dissect their motivations and analyze the ambitions of their hearts. In lieu of that, she'd make it up in her head.

That couple strolling past an old-timey fire engine that had little kids climbing all over it? They'd been in love since puberty and had gotten married the second they were old enough. Rolling with her imagination now, she kept going. Well into their mid-forties now, they were comfortable with each other, but not so much that they'd lost interest. The wife pointed to the roasted cashew booth and he gamely ordered her a sleeveful without blinking an eye. She shared it with him, popping nuts into his mouth with a laugh. It was so sweet that it put a warm glow in Angela's chest.

She wanted that. A man who adored her and could be her friend after the initial rush wore off. One day... maybe.

People thronged the main thoroughfare as Angela guided Fiona through the crowd, keeping a firm grip on her friend's arm. Two men in plaid used a double-handled flat saw to cut wood in half in what appeared to be some kind of contest of skill or speed. Hard to tell.

A dozen or more other activities lined the street, with varying groups of onlookers and participants at each one. Everyone wore smiles and winter coats, perfectly okay with the freezing temperatures in spring.

A large redwood barn held court in the center of the MapleFaire. Angela dragged Fiona inside. Honestly, she'd had a moment when she'd been convinced Fiona would chicken out and refuse to set one foot in MapleFaire. She was *so* messed up over Nate. Goodness knew why. Fiona had a ton of great qualities and any man would be lucky to call her his girlfriend. If Nathanial Boyd couldn't see that, he didn't deserve a second of Fiona's grief.

Easier said than done to convince her friend that she was better off. That she should be using this time to get over the guy. Lots of attractive, available men would be happy to take a successful, beautiful woman to dinner. She got invitations of that sort all the time herself. Too bad none of the men ever held her interest longer than five minutes.

Because, you know...none of them were Brandon Rangely.

And she would bet every last maple tree in Vermont that he'd fall over in shock if someone told him she'd always had a crush on him.

Vendor tables full of maple syrup and fresh vegetables ringed the outside of the barn and more skill games better suited to indoors nestled up cozily in between them. Angela wanted to visit them all.

Twice. She consulted her map. "You know you can get a maple sugar scrub facial here?"

"Wait, you're not going all Vermont on me here, are you?" Fiona asked with her mouth twisted up in dismay.

Angela checked her eye roll because Fiona was her oldest friend, but it was hard. There was nothing wrong with Vermont, but Fiona insisted on talking about the place where her father and brother lived like it had something inherently terrible about it. It didn't. Fiona had transferred her issues with her father to the inn and by extension, Vermont as a whole. But anytime Angela brought it up, she hit a brick wall. So she kept looking for new ways to dismantle it. For Fiona's sake.

Angela threaded around a throng of people and commented casually, "Well, you know, country life sure looks good on your little bro."

Fiona followed her line of vision to a booth where people threw beanbags at targets. Brandon was the one handing out beanbags. Angela had noticed him a split second after walking into the barn and had kept him in her sights because he was beautiful to look at. Always had been. He'd never seemed to return the sentiment, often treating her like an appendage of Fiona's he didn't quite know what to do with.

Look at the greeting she'd gotten back at the inn yesterday. *Trouble twins.* He'd been calling her and Fiona that for two decades. At some point, he should have realized that Angela wasn't ten anymore; she'd earned a masters in psychology and had a thriving practice. Not to mention she kept in shape and updated her wardrobe regularly. Lots of men would be happy to go out with her. Just not the one she *wished* would ask her out.

They watched Brandon clap when a teenage girl knocked over one of the targets, then he handed her a large stuffed monkey with a huge smile that lit up his face.

"Though he's not so little anymore," Ang murmured as she openly checked Brandon out.

He did look good. Much better than she'd recalled. Granted, it had been at least three years since the last time she'd seen him and that had been back in New York. Before he'd jumped ship to help out his dad with the inn.

Fiona quirked a brow at her, cluing her in that her expression probably revealed more than she intended. So what? Though she'd never mentioned her crush to her friend, the odds of Fiona being unaware were zero. They'd been friends too long for anything to be much of a shock between them.

So it shouldn't faze Fiona if Angela ducked out for a minute to see what trouble she could get into while she had Brandon trapped at a carnival game booth, where he couldn't ignore her and couldn't avoid her.

"Be right back," she murmured and skedaddled before Fiona could tell her not to waste her time.

It was Angela's time to waste, wasn't it?

Brandon's expression zeroed in on Angela as she

waltzed up to the beanbag toss and handed him a dollar.

"Hey, stranger," she all but purred.

"Angela."

Brandon tucked the bill into his apron and handed her three beanbags. His fingers grazed hers and she felt it all the way to her toes. Judging by the way he jerked his hand back as if he'd touched an electric fence, he'd felt it too.

Oh, so they were going to pretend that hadn't happened. Noted.

"What's the trick here?" she asked with a wink. "I do want to get my money's worth."

Brandon actually smiled and that hit her in the gut much harder than the accidental brush of his fingers. Who would have seen that coming?

"No trick. Just finesse," he said with a cute shrug. "Let me show you."

Before she could blink, he'd rounded the long counter between them and crowded up behind her, wrapping his hand around hers to demonstrate what was likely supposed to be a tossing technique, but she'd gotten all lost in the scent of pine trees and lemon that seemed to be wafting from him in some kind of masculine treat for the senses.

He flung her hand forward with his, and she managed to loosen her grip on the beanbag. It flew through the air and knocked over all three stacked milk jugs in one shot.

Brandon cheered. She spun in excitement and

got tangled in his feet, falling heavily against him. Glancing up, she froze as his expression darkened. The air fairly crackled with energy as the moment dragged on and on. Carefully, he steadied her with both of his strong hands on her upper arms.

"Easy, there," he murmured, their gazes locked. "Can't have you in a heap on the floor."

She swallowed and then the moment broke as he dropped his hands, stepping back out of her reach. But it didn't matter. He couldn't untouch her, nor pretend that hadn't been a turning point.

He'd seen her. Really opened his eyes and *seen* her as a woman. She could tell. Coming to Vermont had been an inspired move on her part. Now she just had to figure out how to get to the next step with Brandon.

SIX

Ang had abandoned Fiona in favor of her brother and Fiona tried not to be jealous. The more time they spent together, the better, in Fiona's opinion, though it was way too early in the morning to be thinking about Ang and the little brother she'd witnessed eating bugs, dancing naked to the radio and getting scolded for eating his entire plastic pumpkin full of Halloween candy in one night. She glanced in any direction but that one.

And immediately regretted it when she spied Derek.

"Oh, great, look who's here." It was out of Fiona's mouth before she could catch it and, of course, that was when Delia appeared like magic, sliding easily into the spot Ang had vacated.

"Yeah, he's doing a cooking demonstration." Delia waved at no less than a hundred people. Probably it was five. Felt like a hundred. "That's the great thing about living in a small community. You see familiar faces everywhere you turn."

"And the great thing about New York is you can lose yourself in a crowd."

In spite of herself, she couldn't help but wander over to witness Derek in his element. She'd never seen him cook, only sampled the end result. He wore a gray chef's coat with panache, and dang it, he looked good in it.

A small crowd watched as Derek held up a pan, gesturing to it with a syrup bottle.

"So with the scallops golden brown, we pour in some of Vermont's finest maple syrup, and reduce it down..." He swirled the syrup around the pan where thick, whitish-brown disks sizzled. "The maple actually brings out the scallop's own sweetness. And, *voila*, maple-glazed sea scallops."

Derek punctuated that by serving the scallops onto small plates and spooning some of the syrup from the pan over the delicate browned circles.

Wait a minute. "I thought you said you only cooked with locally sourced ingredients," she called to him. "Vermont has no coast. So I'm guessing you went rogue on the sea scallops."

Derek didn't miss a beat and flashed her a smug smile. "I see we have a heckler. This might interest you. At one time, New York and New Hampshire both claimed Vermont, till the Green Mountain Boys defended our land grants. These scallops come from New Hampshire, so how about we make peace and just call them Vermont-Adjacent Scallops?"

Impressed against her will, Fiona asked, "And how do you know all that?"

"My mom's eighth-generation Vermonter."

"And that's a good thing?" she murmured to Delia who didn't hear her. She jetted off after someone with a cry and a wave.

"Pardon the interruption," Derek said to the crowd as he passed out napkins but his gaze was on Fiona. "City folk."

Ang wandered back over from her side jaunt to flirt with Brandon. Fiona used the excuse to move away from the smart-aleck chef. She and Ang left the cooking demo area and wandered into another section of carnival games. "He is so annoying."

It was a shame how that gray coat brought out the silvery blue in his eyes.

"Come on, Fi. Let's at least have some fun," Ang insisted.

A very large man running the balloon pop game heard her and started in on his pitch. "Ladies, step up and take a shot. One dollar will get you one dart. Hit a balloon and win a sweet prize."

He held up a dart in one hand and a stuffed dog in the other, waggling the animal until his mouth flopped open, which made Fiona laugh for some reason.

"Yes, we should play," Ang said, pinging off Fiona's reaction, no doubt. "It'll be a healthy release of aggression."

"I'm not really in the mood." Fiona shook her head. "This whole thing reminds me of Coney Island. Remember when Nate won me that bear?"

"Come on. We're here to relax and have a good time."

To make her life complete, Derek waltzed up carrying a tub of dishes from his demonstration. "Yeah, and there are no two-hundred dollar mani-pedi places here. By the way, you're my ride back to the inn."

"Oh, lucky me," Fiona called after him as he sauntered off. She turned back to the booth. "You know what, Ang. Why not?"

Ang clapped her hands as Fiona handed the operator a dollar in exchange for a dart. She took aim and just as she was about to let it fly, she heard a man's voice behind her. A familiar voice. The dart left her hand at the same moment she turned. That *voice*. It had to be…

Nate. The crowd shifted and there he was. So good looking and solid and so much a sight for sore eyes.

"Nate," she hissed to Ang from the corner of her mouth. "You know what, he must have called my office and followed us up here. I knew he'd change his mind."

Knew it, knew it, knew it! Of course he'd been unable to live without her, pining away day after day as he thought about how much he missed her. How good they'd been together.

"Oh, that is so romantic," Ang breathed with a little misty glint in her eyes.

"Nate," Fiona called, unable to keep the large smile from her face. Thank goodness. This little interlude of singlehood, Vermont and all the heartbreak could be history within five minutes. "Nathanial."

"Fiona." Nate glanced around with a decidedly not-thrilled look on his face. "What are you doing here?"

She faltered. Why was he surprised to see her if he'd followed her here? "Well, I could ask you the same thing."

Before either of them could answer, a pretty blonde girl in a chic hot pink jacket walked right into Nate's personal space and put her hand on his arm. "This place is so much fun, isn't it, Nate?"

Nate's face split into a smile and he put his arm around the interloper. Then he seemed to realize what he was doing and half pulled it back.

Um…what was going on here? Fiona's gaze cut back and forth between the two people, one a total stranger and one who was so familiar that she couldn't stop gaping at him as the tension grew legs, then stomped all over her chest.

"I'm, uh—" Fiona swallowed. "Just so surprised to see you here."

"Nate, honey," Pink Jacket said with extremely wide eyes. "What's up?"

"I just…um, well, I ran into an old friend." Nate flung a hand at Fiona as if someone in this little circle might be confused who he meant.

"That's one way of putting it," Ang commented sweetly.

Fiona shook her head but nothing magically started making sense here. "What's going on?"

Nate's face turned a shade of green as he pointed at Pink Jacket. "This is Hailey. My, um…new girlfriend."

Pink Jacket beamed at him as he committed this time and put his arm around her possessively.

Does not compute. Fiona's brain whirled in a hundred different directions but what came out of her mouth was, "That's so funny, I thought you just said *girlfriend.*"

The word tasted horrific on her tongue and she wanted to spit it out.

Hailey laughed. "He did."

And now it was real. Pink Jacket, Hailey and girlfriend were all titles that belonged to the same person, and it wasn't Fiona. Nate had *not* chased her down, was not suffering from a broken heart. He'd brought a *new girlfriend* to Vermont. Where Fiona was.

"Wow, ah, that was…*fast,*" Fiona managed to return and almost didn't choke on it. "How—how did you two meet?"

"Actually" —Nate nodded at Hailey— "she's a friend of my sister's."

"Hailey," Delia called a moment before she joined the funfest going on here at MapleFaire. "Hailey Summit, I thought that was you."

Nate had the foresight to turn away like the coward he was so Delia didn't recognize him.

"Hi, Mrs. Rangely," Hailey bubbled over with her greeting and Fiona had a feeling that was her default. It was too much.

"I'm sorry," Fiona cut in because this crazy train

needed to pull into the station really darn fast. "Do you two know each other?"

"Oh, sure," Delia said. "Hailey's family has been coming to the inn since it opened." To Hailey, she said, "I have your family's reservation ready; your two favorite rooms as usual."

"Oh, it's not for my family," Hailey corrected and pointed at Nate over her shoulder. "It's for my boyfriend and I. I always loved MapleFaire growing up and I wanted to show Natey my Vermont."

"Natey?" Fiona enunciated quietly to Ang, who shook her head in mutual bemusement instead of gagging like Fiona wanted to.

Nate swung around and faced Delia at last. "Hi, Mrs. Rangely."

Shock took over Delia's face in an instant. "Oh my."

Suddenly, all the dots connected and sliced Fiona across the chest with long sharp hooks. "Wait, you're staying at the *inn*?"

Hailey's gaze darted between them all and finally landed on Nate. "What am I missing here?"

"It's a really small world," Fiona told her in no uncertain terms. "And it just got a whole lot smaller. I'm Fiona."

"Hi, Fiona." Hailey smiled. And then it registered and she flinched. "Oh."

"Yeah, oh," Fiona repeated, and because none of this humiliation could possibly be complete without Derek, he strolled by to stick his nose into the crazy.

"Hey," he said to Fiona. "Tick tock. I gotta get dinner started."

The timely out seemed like a lifeline all at once. Thank goodness. She could bail on this scene with a ready excuse. Except Nate was still focused on her like he had something else to say and she couldn't wait to hear what it was. "One sec."

Derek nodded and kept strolling toward his demo station.

Nate spread his hands. "This is the last place I expected you to be."

"At her dad's?" Ang threw in sarcastically and Fiona shot her a grateful look. That woman had her back and Fiona really appreciated it at this moment.

"Away from the city," Nate corrected and it was a fair point. Not that Fiona was handing him any. She crossed her arms and glared at him. "Look, I had no idea it was your dad's place. We can stay at another inn."

The look Hailey shot him said she thought differently and then Delia shook her head. "It's MapleFaire. I doubt there will be any vacancies between here and Montpelier."

No, of course not. That would be too kind of the universe to arrange for her.

"I'm so sorry, Fiona," Nate said. "I didn't mean for this to happen."

"It's fine." Fiona waved it off, pleased that her voice didn't waver at all. Why would it? She got the message.

Nate had moved on. Nothing to see here. Fiona could put this all behind her.

Just as soon as she made sure Nate really got the point that she was over him. So over him. In fact... she could be dating someone new too. She *should*. She should be dating every eligible male in the place, like... Derek.

He was cute. Look at him over there being all obsessive-compulsive about his cookware as he packed it up. Derek was an accomplished chef and...and could chop wood like a pro. He grew things. He was great.

"Really?" Nate asked.

"Sure, it's totally fine." Fiona glanced at Ang and then completely lost control of her mouth. "Because I'm also actually seeing someone new too."

Oh, goodness. What had possessed her to say that? Thinking it and saying it were two totally different things and now it was out there. She couldn't take it back.

Ang's frozen smile didn't help sell that idea but Nate wasn't looking at Angela. He was blinking at Fiona as if he couldn't quite process her statement. "You...you are?"

"Yeah," Fiona said brightly and glanced at Derek as the threads of this totally stupid or completely brilliant plan unspooled in her mind. "Well, he's the executive chef at the inn. And he's just a great guy. You guys would love him. He's really talented—"

"Hey." Derek's voice rang out over the crowd. "Come on. Who scratched my crepe pan?"

"He's a little temperamental, but that comes with being a genius," Fiona told Hailey who was listening raptly, a ditzy smile on her face. Clearly, she still believed in Santa and that every cloud had a silver lining. Next, Fiona would try to sell the woman a bridge. "He sources everything locally, can you believe that? Well, everything except for me, of course."

She gave a dainty shrug as Delia and Ang stared at her as if she'd grown two heads. But she couldn't back down now. Nate swallowed twice and shot Derek a covert once-over out of the corner of his eye. That put a warm little thrill in Fiona's midsection.

Take that, Nate. Not so much fun to have it rubbed in your face that someone you used to date has moved on, is it?

The glow of having put Nate in his place lasted until she and Ang got back to their room, when Fiona started throwing clothes into a suitcase. Packing would take no time at all if she didn't fold anything, didn't look up and didn't cry. Easier said than done.

Nate had *moved on.* Moved on so fast that he was already at the girlfriend-label stage.

Ang stood by the fireplace, her psychologist hat firmly in place as she eyed Fiona. "I don't get it. I mean, what were you thinking?"

"I wasn't, okay?" Fiona dumped some underwear into the suitcase and dashed back to another drawer. "I clearly have maple syrup on the brain. But I have the perfect fix for all of this. We leave."

Where was her other suitcase? There, on the dresser.

Ugh, this whole thing had her all turned around. But now she had a plan and going back to the city was it. She grabbed the suitcase and hauled it to the bed.

"I mean," she said to Ang. "You're welcome to stay if you want. But the universe is clearly telling me that Vermont and I do not mix."

"Fi, don't you see that if you leave now, it'll look like you still care." Ang put her hand on one of the posts of the bed, leaning into her argument.

That was achingly true. What was she supposed to do, sit around the inn and watch Nate and Pink Jacket play kissy face? Fiona zipped a suitcase closed. "I know, but I can't do this."

"It's just one night until Delia finds someplace else for them to stay."

"That's one night too many." She shouldered a bag and grabbed her two suitcases. Hopefully she had everything. If not, Delia could send whatever she'd forgotten. "If you're coming with me, meet me at the car."

Somehow, she made it down the stairs with all of her luggage and without breaking a leg. Naturally, the moment she hit the ground floor, Nate materialized in front of her, his handsome face earnest and searching.

"Going somewhere?" he asked.

Caught, Fiona lied. "No. Why would you think that?"

The suitcases and her breakneck speed maybe? But he didn't call her on it. "So listen, I'm really sorry about all of this. It's just going to be for one night."

"Please." Fiona dismissed that with a wave. "It's fine. Whatever. I mean, you sure did meet Hailey fast."

That had come out far too forlorn. Not doing so hot in convincing Nate she'd moved on too, which was paramount. It wouldn't do for him to think she was so needy.

"Yeah. The timing just worked out." His gaze hadn't left Fiona's face one time. "You too. With that chef, huh?"

"Oh, Derek." Fiona tried on a dreamy face as if the very name filled her with bliss instead of the complicated thing they had going on now where one minute she grudgingly liked him and the next minute she wanted to bonk him on the head with his sauté pan. "Yeah, that was just…lightning bolts, you know?"

"Great." Nate smiled, looking so much like his old self that she nearly wept. "That's really great. It is really good to see you again."

There was a long pause and their gazes met, drawing out the connection. He put his hand on her arm, almost like old times. And then he seemed to remember that they were broken up and he shouldn't be touching her. His arm dropped back to his side and his expression grew uncomfortable. "I have to go meet Hailey down at the lake. I'll see you around."

That had been…interesting. Not like he was over her at all. She watched him go, barely squelching the urge to call him back. A familiar voice over her shoulder killed it instantly.

"Fiona," Derek called smoothly from the kitchen.

Turning slowly, she saw him leaning on the doorframe, arms crossed and his usual smirk spread across his jaw. "A word?"

It wasn't a request. He'd clearly heard everything and he was calling her on the carpet. Perfect. Just when all of this couldn't get any worse, it did.

SEVEN

Derek picked up the dishes he'd been about to hand wash when he overheard Fiona's big confession in the foyer. "So. I hear we're an item."

That was an interesting twist he hadn't seen coming. She hadn't picked him by chance. How much of it was motivated by the attraction that had flared up between them in the greenhouse earlier, the one he'd deny if anyone pressed him on it?

"Oh. You heard that?" Fiona asked with a little gasp, like there was something wrong with his hearing. "I am so sorry. It just slipped out. Nate and I, we just broke up a few weeks ago and he already has a new girlfriend up here."

Wow. Nice. He put the dishes into the sink and decided to do them later. This conversation had just gotten way too complicated for running water. "A few weeks?"

"Twenty-three days and seven hours. Ish." Fiona shrugged.

"Pretty quick for a rebound. Not much of a

gentleman." There were rules about that sort of thing. You had to give yourself a mourning period. Of course, his was going on two years, but who was counting?

Fiona, apparently. She knew the breakup day down to the hour. Which meant she was still hurting from it, so he gave her a pass on lying to her ex about the status of their relationship. Clearly, she'd wanted to make him jealous and he couldn't fault her for that, either.

"Yeah, but I think we just had a moment," she said breathlessly, a gleam stealing into her eye.

Wait, did she mean with *Nate*? Maybe she hadn't felt that bit of heat with Derek earlier. His ego might be a little crushed, which put him in a not-so-charitable mood all at once. "A moment of delusion?"

"No, a spark." She batted her eyes at him. "I need your help. Pretend to be my boyfriend for the week."

Pretend? Derek didn't do pretend, not with women. Not after Lizette. His girlfriend in France had been living a double life—married and seeing Derek on the side. "Let me think about that. No."

"Please let me save a little dignity here," she begged.

Cabbage in each hand, he turned back to the crazy woman who had invaded his kitchen. "No, I've got MapleFaire this week and the food bloggers are coming. And even if I was as delusional as you are, which I'm not, there's nothing in it for me."

That sounded way more mercenary than intended but she'd struck a nerve with her pretend-boyfriend spiel. He'd already been a pretend boyfriend once, thanks.

"How about a quid pro quo?" Fiona suggested. "You want that field for your organic farm, right?"

"Of course. I'd have vegetables farm to table in minutes instead of days. It'd be a dream. But a pipe dream. Chauncey will never go for it."

"Your dream is farm to table? I can get that for you."

The cabbages in his hands came from upstate. As he chopped them, he pondered how much nicer it would be if they could have come from down the lane. He could watch them grow, nurture them. The vision took hold and it was tough to get it out of his head.

But he had to—reality was reality. "Not likely. Chauncey is a classic New Englander. He hates change and the city people he thinks this inn is attracting."

The gleam in Fiona's eye turned crafty. "He's just positioning himself for a better offer."

"Oh, no." Derek laughed. You could take the girl out of the city, but not the city out of the girl. "Look, up here, money isn't always the deciding factor. Chauncey isn't some Wall Street type buying up co-ops in SoHo."

Somehow he'd leaned into her space and they were nearly nose to nose. She didn't back down and oh, yes, there was definitely some heat here whether she wanted to admit it or not.

She was into this pretend-boyfriend idea, and he had an unhealthy dose of curiosity whether his part in it had any relevance to how bad she wanted to make it happen. And she wanted it badly, that was for sure.

It was all over her posture, the fierce determination in her expression.

"Okay, listen," she said. "I have sold a closet with no windows. I have bought a Tribeca loft for a song. You want that field? I'll get it for you."

"Impossible." Now he was just baiting her. Because it was fun.

"Not in my vocabulary," Fiona singsonged back.

He held back the scoff. Barely. And then he realized she wasn't joking. "You're serious. For the field?"

"Yep."

He stared at her for a long moment. And he must be as crazy as her because he couldn't stop himself from nodding. "Looks like you got yourself a pretend boyfriend for the week."

They shook on it and the zing of their clasped hands went all the way up his arm.

What was wrong with him that he just really wanted to see what happened? It wasn't like Lizette, not really. Everyone knew the score here and they'd be going their separate ways at the end of the week, no harm, no foul. Nate the Loser got a taste of his own medicine.

And just maybe Fiona might make good on her part of the bargain. He wasn't going to count on her getting that field—he had way too much sense for that. But a guy could dream, right?

After an extremely restful night, Fiona came downstairs bright and early the next morning, and ran into her dad in the reception area.

"Hey," he called. "Morning, kiddo. You look nice."

"Thanks, Dad." She couldn't help but smile. Maybe they weren't in such a bad place after all if they could be this genuine with each other.

"Listen, I've been on the phone all morning. Every hotel, motel and inn in the county is booked solid. I'm sorry, honey." Her father put his hand on her arm earnestly. "If you want me to ask Hailey and Nate to leave, I will."

"No, no," Fiona protested. "It's fine."

It was totally fine. Derek had signed on for the fake boyfriend role—somehow—and that only worked if the target stayed here. Somehow she had to segue this plan into something workable, if for no other reason than to save face. But if she did it right, there was always the possibility of getting Nate back. It could happen.

"You sure?"

"Yeah, listen. Has Nate been down this morning?" She and Derek needed to get started faking it up in front of Nate and there was no time like the present.

Harris shrugged. "Sure, he and Hailey went for a morning walk in the woods. Why?"

"Oh, no reason."

"So you're okay?"

Fiona's throat got a little tight. Her dad seemed so concerned about fixing this problem that wasn't his to resolve. It was…nice. As long as they didn't talk about the elephant in the inn, namely that it existed, then things were cool. She'd remember that.

But first, she and Derek had a walk to take.

She strode into the kitchen where he washed dishes in the sink. The blue chambray shirt he wore fit him really nicely and he'd rolled the sleeves up to his elbows, which was a lot more attractive than she'd have guessed. Maybe because it was already nice to witness a man wash dishes.

"Missed breakfast but there's still some brioche left," he called without turning around.

He knew the sound of her walk already? That brought her up short. For half a second. Time was wasting. "Never mind that. They're on a romantic stroll, which means we are too."

"But the dishes."

"That can wait. Come on," she insisted. "Meet me outside in five minutes."

He sighed. "Yes, dear."

But Fiona was almost too far away to hear him. She was definitely too far away to see the smirk on his face, but she knew it was there just based on his tone. She didn't care. This was going to work. She hoped. Actually, she wasn't quite sure what the definition of "work" would be. One step at a time. If they ran into Nate and Hailey, and she intended to be sure they did, she could feel out the situation and figure out the best next move.

As long as Nate was good and jealous, saw that

he'd given up something great, and ditched Hailey, that would be okay with Fiona. Her heart wouldn't feel so torn anymore.

So next time, Derek would get some things in writing, like what a "walk" meant to Fast and Furious Fiona. She outpaced him all the way down the slope at the east end of the house, despite him being the one wearing appropriate footwear.

"I thought this was supposed to be a romantic stroll, not a sprint," he called after her.

"At this pace, they'll be back before we get started." She glanced at his feet. "What's with those shoes?"

"What's wrong with my duck boots?" They happened to be good for walking in snow, which currently covered the ground an inch thick.

"Where do I start?" Fiona muttered and then as if to prove his point, she slid on a patch of ice, forcing Derek to grab her arm.

Fortunately, he was able to keep them both off the ground. "This is Vermont. I have a pair for you if you want them."

"Please. I'm trying to win him back, not scare him away."

Oh. So that was the goal. Not just jealousy, but the whole nine yards. This should be fairly entertaining then. Derek shoved back a totally misplaced furl of disappointment. Fiona had never said she'd picked him to be her fake boyfriend because she liked him. In fact, they were constantly at odds, with her big mouth and speed demon tendencies. No big deal.

"You're going to regret it," he told her just as she stepped in a particularly large patch of mud.

Her high-heeled boot sank into the mire almost to the ankle. She squealed and flailed around, but she was stuck. Derek to the rescue. He swung an arm around her and lifted her at the knees with his other one. Her foot came out of the boot, leaving it in the mud and her with one sock-covered foot.

Of course she couldn't settle down and let him play knight in shining armor. She twisted around like a stuck pig who didn't have sense enough to know that the more you struggled, the harder it was to get free.

"What are you doing?" she protested. "Put me down."

"Quit wiggling. You're going to put us both in the mud." Which would be a shame because she felt nice in his arms.

"Put me down!" she demanded and almost rolled free anyway, so he granted her wish, dropping her right where they stood. Back into the mud. Her bare foot sank way deeper than it had when she'd been wearing boots.

She blasted him with a furious glare. "I didn't say put me down right here."

Oh, well, forgive me for not being a mind reader. But just as Derek was about to help her out, totally against his better judgment, mind you, they got some company.

"Having some trouble, there?" Nate called.

Derek looked up to see Fiona's ex and his new girlfriend approaching, arm in arm as if they actually understood the concept of a romantic stroll. Must be nice. Derek composed his face because this was what he'd signed up for. Showtime.

"Oh, no, no," Fiona exclaimed brightly and bent over to pull her boot from the mud. "We're fine. Hi."

She strung out that one word to about eighteen syllables and tucked her hair behind an ear with a fake smile to match her fake relationship. Derek rolled his eyes.

Hailey snuggled closer to her man on the rebound. "We were just out for a walk."

Boy, she was a perky one. Nate, for his part, zeroed in on Derek, sizing him up with a measured glance.

"We haven't formally met," he said pointing his index finger at Derek in a classic gun position. It wasn't hard to see that he felt a whole lot threatened by Derek's presence.

Fiona piped up. "Sorry. Nate, Hailey, this is Derek."

Nate uncurled his fingers from the gun shape and shook Derek's hand. With a smile, Derek squeezed as hard as he could, which was saying something given that his primary workout included chopping wood. You let your hold slip on the axe, you got hurt. So he never slipped.

"That's quite the grip you got there," Nate commented as he peered up at Derek.

There was not one blessed thing wrong with being a little smug about the fact that he topped Nate by six inches, so Derek reveled in it, along with the reddened places along the loser's palm when he pulled it back.

"You two are so cute together," Hailey exclaimed. Bubbly might as well have been her middle name. "How'd you two meet?"

Curveball alert. Alarms sounded in Derek's head as he scrambled for a coherent thought. He glanced at Fiona, at a total loss. Had she already concocted a story? Fake dating wasn't his forte, at least not the kind where he was aware of it. "We, uh…"

"I…I was up visiting the inn and we sort of just bumped into each other," Fiona broke in and smiled up at him adoringly.

It should have warmed him up, but that wasn't the Fiona he was used to. Besides, it was too fake. This whole plan could go anytime. He liked her better when she was being sassy.

"Literally," Derek added with a laugh, because he could envision that perfectly. Fiona on her phone, not paying attention. Unsuspecting Vermont boy at the wheel… "City drivers, right? Always speeding."

"Well, yeah, but—" Fiona continued in a rush to get her side on the record. "He was driving dangerously under the speed limit."

"You know how hard it is to get Fiona to slow down," he countered with a fake smile of his own that had a few pointed barbs in it just for her.

"Maybe I don't need to slow down; maybe you

91

need to speed up," she suggested sweetly and that was more like it. That honest, spitfire woman he knew how to handle.

He had to chuckle as he slung an arm around her and pulled her into his side. "And it just came together in a fender bender of love."

"Wow," Nate commented, looking a little dazed.

He knew the feeling. Derek was done with this kind of fun. Too much to keep track of, too many moving parts. "We're off for a nice relaxing walk in the woods. Isn't that right, Fiona?"

And then he made the mistake of staring down into her eyes and their close proximity became increasingly apparent. He wouldn't have minded if they actually were planning to take a walk together, because they were a couple and wanted to spend time together.

Or rather, he wished he could find a woman like that. Not Fiona necessarily. Just… someone special who wasn't faking their relationship.

Another pipe dream. Such a woman didn't exist. And Fiona was the fakest of the fake. They didn't even like each other. But Nate didn't have to know that.

"She loves to slow down now," Derek managed to get out. "Isn't that right, honey?"

"I do," she crooned, glancing up at him with another adoring smile, and all at once, he forgot it was fake. He couldn't get that sudden vision out of his head of how things would work between them if she really did slow down long enough to see what he had to offer.

He did like her sassy mouth and the way she said what she meant. The way she ate his cinnamon rolls and how she threw herself into everything she— What was he *doing*? No. Just no. He did not appreciate any of those things.

"Okay," Nate said and glanced at Hailey for the first time since they'd walked up, which told Derek a whole bunch about the state of things. "Maybe we'll see you at MapleFaire."

"Yeah, maybe," Derek said and as the couple walked off, he called out, "Nice to meet you."

"Bye." Fiona waited until the couple had strolled a good fifty yards and then she wrenched out of his embrace with a smack to his arm. "What are you doing?"

Why had he expected *thank you* to be the first words out of her mouth? Glutton for punishment all right; that was his row to hoe. "I thought that was good."

"No, it was a little too much."

"Here, let me give you a hand." He reached for her boot and she pushed him back.

"You've been helpful enough. Thanks for the help."

Even when she did say thanks, she loaded it with enough sarcasm that it was clearly not meant to be actual gratitude. Why was he putting up with this again? Certainly wasn't for her charming personality or even the field. The odds of her getting Chauncey to budge were slim. Might be time to look in the mirror and figure out what he was really getting out of this deal other than grief.

When they reached the landing outside the front door, he heard the Rangelys talking inside, which put the icing on the crazy cake.

"Where's Derek?" Harris called out. "The kitchen's a mess. That's so unlike him."

Delia, who must have been sitting at her desk, said, "I believe that he's out on a stroll with Fiona."

"What? Why?" Harris asked, his confusion carrying through the very walls of the house. That made two of them wondering the same thing.

"Because they're dating now, dear," she commented mildly.

"Mock dating," another female voice threw in. Probably Angela, Fiona's friend, and he silently thanked her for the distinction, one everyone needed to keep in the forefront of their minds. Especially himself.

Fiona, who still stood on this side of the front door alongside him, acted like she hadn't heard any of it, probably because she wasn't employed here. What did it matter to her if anyone questioned his work ethic?

"Well, see you later," she said casually.

"Whoa, that's it?" Derek couldn't believe he wasn't letting her go. He should. He should get as far away from Fiona Rangely as possible. But he couldn't forget how stymied Nate had been to see the two of them together. It gave Derek a sense of satisfaction he'd rather not examine to have something the Loser wanted.

Fiona needed to step it up a notch while they had Nate's attention or she had no prayer of this fake relationship working. Was he seriously the only one who saw that?

"Well, yeah," she said. "I've got contracts to look at this morning."

"You don't want to make it seem like you're hiding out in your room away from Nate."

That got her attention. She swung around to face him. "No. Of course not."

"Everyone in town is going to MapleFaire today, including us." He held out a crooked arm for her to take. Which she did with an exasperated noise in her throat.

"I guess I'm just going to have to enjoy myself on this trip or die trying."

That's the spirit, he almost said but she opened the door to drag him inside before he could get it out. She'd never slow down. Why he'd even said that earlier remained a mystery.

Fiona caught sight of the small crowd in the reception area and invited her brother and Angela to go with them to MapleFaire. They both immediately agreed and went to get their coats.

"What is going on here?" Harris sputtered as all his help walked out of the room.

But not before Derek heard Delia respond. "Spring is in the air."

Clearly it had affected all of them in more ways than one.

EIGHT

MapleFaire day two had little to differentiate it from day one, except for the heightened vibe in the air, as if the fairgoers had caught a bit of the spirit. The crowd thronged around Fiona and Derek as they strolled between carnival games and soft pretzel carts. Ang and Brandon had run off to get portraits drawn.

Without the sure thing of running into Nate and Hailey, Fiona was at loose ends. She couldn't quite figure out where to put her hands. Derek had somehow moved extra close to her side, probably because of the crush of people, but it felt like... more. Ever since he'd picked her up, she had this awareness of him she couldn't shake.

Wow, did he have some solid arms. They were currently hidden by his winter coat, but she'd gotten a peek at them earlier when he'd been washing dishes. Coupled with the fact that he'd hefted her easily, scarcely without losing his breath—that was something else.

And somehow, he'd gotten her to *stroll*. She didn't think she'd ever strolled before.

But apparently it was how you stimulated conversation, since that seemed to be what they were currently doing. Small talk and strolling. Madness.

Instead of doing MapleFaire 2.0, she should have taken the out she'd given herself with those contracts and hightailed it to her room earlier. Away from Derek. She couldn't stop thinking about how that morning walk had shifted from a mechanism to make Nate jealous into something else.

What, she had no idea.

"I love the smell of maple syrup in the morning," Derek commented casually as they passed dual fire pits surrounded by hay bales. "So. You grew up in Manhattan. Let me guess. Hell's Kitchen?"

"No, Upper West Side near the park. More like Hell's Breakfast Nook."

"Chauncey," Derek said pleasantly and Fiona looked up to see the grizzled old man leading a lowing cow by a braided blue rope, right through the middle of the fair.

"Hi, sir," she added with a wave. True to form, he looked right through them and aimed the cow in the other direction. As she watched him meander off, she glanced at Derek. "That guy is allergic to hellos."

"Just don't forget your end of the bargain," Derek supplied helpfully, like she'd forget.

Why did he think she'd been nice to the old man? She had this. Or rather, she would. "I know."

She started to reel off some ideas for how she'd get him that field when Derek interrupted her.

"Ex-boyfriend sighting, one o'clock," he murmured as they entered the wide open air barn with a long banner that read "27th Annual Pancake Eating Contest" in swirly font.

Sneaking a peek in that direction, Fiona spotted them easily. You could pick out Hailey's pink jacket while blindfolded. "Ugh, they're sharing a candied apple."

Hailey picked off little bits and fed them to Nate. It was disgusting how sweet they were with each other. Nate had never been like that with Fiona, not that she'd wanted him to be. They'd been too busy to sit around and do lovey-dovey couple things.

Wait. Had he wished they'd done lovey-dovey couple things? Was that why he'd dumped her? A heads-up would have been nice. *Hey, Fiona, let's share a candied apple.* Not rocket science, Nate.

She couldn't stop watching them. Until Derek said, "Two can play that game."

Fiona swung around to see Derek purchasing a cone topped with a cloud of blue cotton candy. Nice. And unexpected. Derek didn't wait around for his girlfriend to call the shots; he just took charge, and decisiveness was far more attractive than she'd have guessed. "Oh. You sure know how to spoil a girl."

When he handed it to her, their fingers brushed and the smile blooming on her face felt far more genuine than she'd have expected. Slowing down had its merits.

"Hey," Derek said, his voice dropping a little into an interesting husky realm. "What kind of fake boyfriend do you take me for?"

There wasn't a trace of his usual smirk and it struck her that he was really, really good looking. Tall, brown-haired and all-American. An accomplished chef. All at once, she had a burning curiosity to know if this would be how he'd treat her if he was a real boyfriend. If so, there was a lot to recommend Derek Price to the female population.

"Okay, so we've got pickled jalapeños, capers and peppers," he informed her. "Or…ooh, you could bob for apples, or how about a little country karaoke up there on the stage—"

"You really enjoy putting me in awkward situations, don't you?" She tried to put a little sarcasm in her voice, but it didn't come out that way. Her smile might have something to do with that. This was nice. *He* was nice, when he wasn't being a smart-aleck.

"Of course. It's part of the fun of this whole thing."

They shared another long look, laden with something she couldn't quite put a finger on. They grated on each other's nerves. Except somewhere along the way, that had fallen apart, and now they understood each other. They were in this together, through thick and thin. The shower of sparks inside her tummy was a whole lot better than nice.

All at once, she caught Nate staring at them

from the corner of her eye. "Did you see that?" she whispered. "Nate just peeked over at us. That is called a tell. It's when that buyer takes one long last look at the house, and you know you hooked 'em."

"All right." Derek's expression grew crafty. "We need to up our stakes then. You wanna make him jealous, right?"

"Of course," she said automatically, though in the last few minutes, she'd lost sight of what she'd been trying to accomplish here. Derek's deep silvery eyes were making her stupid.

"Then we need to look like we're having more fun than they are."

Derek pulled off a gauzy bit of blue cotton candy and stuck it in her mouth. She laughed and let him, the sweet spun concoction melting on her tongue. "You have such a good point."

The interesting thing was that she'd already been having fun. No acting required.

Nate and Hailey sat down at the pancake eating table, side by side as if they couldn't stand to be apart for even a second. What had Derek said earlier? *Two can play that game.* Fiona grabbed Derek and dragged him along with her to the same table. "I hope you brought your appetite."

Derek sank onto the bench. "You know French crêpes, Indian dosas, Ethiopian injera, even blinis in Russia, they all fall under the same delightful banner—pancakes."

The hostess set down a platter full of them in front

of Derek. They were carb-laden, golden brown and delicious looking.

"Save your mouth for eating, honey," Fiona advised him with a little pat to his chest that she made sure Nate saw.

A bald-headed man with round glasses got up on a raised wooden platform and tapped his mic, which emitted a loud squeal over the loudspeaker. The crowd quieted down immediately.

"I'm Mayor Slone, and I'd like to welcome you all. Okay, maple lovers, you each have a plate of eleven pancakes topped with the finest Vermont maple syrup. And whoever eats the most in sixty seconds will be crowned our pancake king or queen!"

Kitschy. But the crowd seemed to love it, swarming over to get front row seats for the action. The contestants picked up their forks, ready to dive in. Derek's complexion started looking a little green but standing behind him, Fiona couldn't really tell. He might be fine.

"Ready?" Mayor Slone called. "Steady. Eat!"

Knives cut into the stacks and forks stabbed triangles of pancake. Everyone at the table shoveled the bits into their mouth. Except Derek, of course, who'd never met a task he couldn't drag out. As if he'd caught slow-motion disease, Derek sliced through his pancakes one at a time, almost delicately.

"What are you doing?" Fiona asked impatiently. Didn't he know how eating contests worked? The mayor had *just* explained it. And Nate's stack had already half disappeared.

"Eating," he said casually.

"At the pace of a field mouse?" she shot back.

"Food is meant to be savored." He glanced over his shoulder at her and popped a small bite into his mouth. "Not endured. Stop pressuring me."

"It's a contest." One that her "boyfriend" was going to lose if he didn't step it up. What kind of message did that send to Nate? *I picked the guy who doesn't understand speed as a winning strategy.*

"Can't do it," he said with a grin. "This needs a little more syrup."

With that, she lost it. Shoving him aside, she said, "Watch out."

Someone had to eat these pancakes. Nate was over there chowing down and he was going to *win* if she didn't turn this ship around. He caught sight of her plan and shoveled his fork faster. Fiona dropped hers and started eating with both hands. The crowd whistled and hooted, cheering for their selected contestants, but it egged her on.

The next thing she knew, both she and Derek were being escorted from the table before the contest had finished. Something about some rules that she'd broken by taking over the eating part from the original contestant. Arguing with the judge didn't help.

Once the judge had deposited them well outside the pancake arena, Fiona smacked the exposed beam railing that marked off the perimeter. "Disqualified. From a pancake-eating competition."

Disqualified. She'd never been disqualified

for anything in her life. Rules were meant to be manipulated in your favor; otherwise co-ops would prevent anyone from buying or selling real estate in Manhattan.

"What, you're blaming me?" Derek protested. "You're the one who stole my pancakes."

"What choice did you leave me?" They were a better couple than Nate and Hailey and winning that contest would have proven it.

"Look," Derek said calmly. "We obviously have different approaches to problem solving."

"Yeah, you're left brained, as in you left your brain at cooking school, and I'm right brained, as in you know I'm right."

Derek smirked at her. That set her back a second. It was the first time that look had made an appearance all day. When had that stopped being his default around her? Maybe it had never been his default. More likely, she'd brought it out in him by being witchy about the contest, when in truth, it wasn't really his fault they'd gotten eliminated.

She'd done that with her insecurities. But geez, it was so hard to see Nate with Hailey. Her gaze wandered to the couple involuntarily and they were both watching her and Derek.

"Oh, no," she muttered and cut her gaze back to Derek. "They're staring at us. We can't be seen arguing. Do something, please."

With literally no warning, Derek leaned forward, gripped her waist and laid his lips on hers. The shock of his mouth startled her and she flinched, knocking their foreheads together.

"What are you doing?" She rubbed at her head, staring at him, trying to get her galloping pulse under control.

"I panicked," he shot back.

Her lips tingled and all she could think about was the fact that she'd just kissed Derek.

But not really. It hadn't been nearly enough to find out what kind of kisser he was, and now she had an unquenchable curiosity. And she didn't want to be thinking about that, not with Nate sitting there watching them.

Her confusion grew. If her goal had been to make Nate jealous, kissing Derek would accomplish that. Wouldn't it? Why hadn't she really played it up, drawn out the kiss? That would have been stellar for her plans.

Well, she knew why. She couldn't because it had felt too real. Derek's hands on her waist had been strong and capable. But—shocker—he had the softest lips. He was so solid and smelled like the best combination of outdoors and sugar and savory herbs.

Nate and Hailey chose that moment to get up from the pancake eating table and exit stage left, probably because they felt sorry for Fiona and her boyfriend, who were clearly not a lovey-dovey couple like them. It was embarrassing for everyone.

"I should just give up and go back to New York,"

she said, her voice betraying how perilously close to tears she was.

"You still owe me a field, remember?" His voice had taken on a bored edge as if he'd been over this whole scene for some time and couldn't wait to get out of here.

"Yes, how could I possibly forget?" she told him with a fake smile designed to get them back on familiar ground—they didn't like each other and this was all pretend. "The sooner the better."

As she strode off, he called out after her, "You even kiss too fast."

And it was a testament to how befuddled he'd made her that of all the things he'd tried to convince her she should slow down and enjoy, kissing was the one she could easily see herself taking him up on.

A minor miracle occurred when Fiona left the pancake-eating barn to see the very person she'd been looking for. Chauncey led his cow on a string right past her. Great timing.

"Mr. Chauncey! Hi. I'm Fiona." It was like talking to a brick wall for all the animation this character had. Did he even hear her? "Here's my card. That's a really great cow you have there."

"It's a steer," he corrected gruffly, but he took the card, so win all the way around.

Rule number one. Always appeal to the seller at his level. "Oh. Well, it's an amazing one."

"Flattery will get you nowhere," he intoned while staring at her card, a hint of derision creeping up around his mouth. He handed the business card back to her. "And I know who you are. Your father runs the inn."

"Yeah." She smiled and prayed it didn't look as forced as it felt. *For the field.* Because she needed to go back to the city and never see Derek again. Immediately. "We're neighbors. I was hoping we could talk neighbor to neighbor about your property for sale."

He shifted from foot to foot and the cow…steer, whatever—who could tell the difference?—got in on that action, swinging his head in time with Chauncey's agitation. Steers didn't trample people, did they?

"What's your interest in it?" Chauncey asked after the steer got good and restless.

"I'm actually inquiring for Derek," she said pleasantly, keeping her eye on the rope around the steer's neck. It looked like Chauncey had a good grip on it. But what did she know?

Chauncey chuckled and stuck a gloved hand on his hip. "Oh, so he's bringing in the big New York guns, huh?"

"I don't know about that, but he's offered you a really fair price." *Come on. Take the offer.* What was the big deal? Buyer and seller, coming together here the same way they had since the dawn of property possession. Money changed hands; everyone was happy.

"Well, you can tell that fellow that I am still not selling to him. Not now, not ever. And that's that."

Chauncey pulled on the blue corded rope attached to his steer's harness and meandered away, leaving Fiona sputtering. "Sir? Sir, maybe we could—"

But he didn't even look back, just kept walking away as if she wasn't still talking. The steer mooed loudly and that put the cap on her day nicely. Of course the animal got the last word.

What in the name of all that was holy did that man have against selling a field to Derek? Sure he was cocky and smug. But with dollars at stake, everyone could put their personal prejudices aside, right?

As she watched him weave between MapleFaire goers, she narrowed her eyes. That field was changing hands with her name on the contract, period, end of story. Chauncey just didn't know it yet.

NINE

Derek stopped the truck about a mile and a half from the inn, parking off the road a bit in case anyone came through here, though odds were pretty slim they'd see another soul. He visited this thatch of woods on a pretty regular basis, just to commune with nature, clear his head. Relax.

After the shenanigans at MapleFaire, he could use all of the above.

Fiona jumped out of the truck, her face buried in her phone. He'd bet a million dollars she still didn't have a signal but she desperately tapped at the screen anyway. He rolled his eyes as he got out and went to lean on the truck bed. Her dependence on being plugged in boggled the mind. But if she'd put that thing down and look around, she might figure out what she was missing—such as the fact that Nate wasn't worth her time.

And maybe Derek was. Sure, he had a bit of ego to fluff up here. But really, this whole fake boyfriend idea had been flawed from the start. Nate was an idiot and he deserved someone as vapid as Hailey. What did Fiona see in that jerk anyway?

Yet another thing he could point out if she'd look up once in a while. "Well," he said brightly. "This morning could have gone better."

"That much we agree on," she said, her gaze tracking her thumbs as she texted something to someone.

"Do you ever slow down?" Stupid question. But he couldn't help ask. She'd gotten him good and intrigued with that millisecond of a kiss. It shouldn't have gone off like that, so awkward and so quickly over.

He might be a little bit fixated on a repeat. Just to see what would happen if he could get her to slow down. It wasn't a crime to wonder.

"Do you ever speed up?" she lobbed back, her thumbs dancing over the screen. It was downright mesmerizing.

"A lot of good things can come from slowing down." He rested his forearms on the bed of the truck, focusing on her pretty face as she scrunched it up in response to whatever was happening in her virtual world.

"Name one."

"Art, for one. Russian novelists. All they needed was a pen and a long winter." She'd barely glanced up for a half a second during this entire conversation, and okay, it sat on his ego like a ton of bricks. "Why do you feel the need to constantly distract yourself?"

"Shh. Give me one second." She looked around for the first time, taking in the miles of snow and trees surrounding them. "Um, what are we doing here?"

He nearly laughed. They'd been parked in this spot for five minutes and she'd just now realized they weren't at the inn. Classic. He hefted a pair of boots, a bucket and a tree tap from the bed of the truck. "I want to show you something. Come on."

This was something he'd never shown anyone before. Why he'd picked Fiona, he couldn't quite say. But there was something growing between them and he wasn't going to apologize for wanting to expand it. Explore it. Take Nate out of the equation and just have something real between them. For once.

"Oh, no no no," Fiona protested. "Where are we going? What are we doing?"

Geez, her mouth did not stop moving. "We're just taking a little field trip."

"After our last walk, I think I just need a hot bath and a book."

"I promise it's going to be worth it this time. But," he threw in and lifted the duck boots he'd pulled from the truck. "You may want to wear these."

She eyed them and would wonders never cease? She sighed and grabbed them. "Fine."

It was a huge concession and he didn't bother to hide his smile. First time in memory she'd taken his advice. He savored the victory in silence and led her into the forest of thick tree trunks, all silent and leafless. The woods during this time of year had a hush that couldn't be replicated indoors, no matter how quiet it got. He loved being out here. Maybe Fiona would too.

Not likely. He glanced at her, but she'd fallen quiet as she trudged along behind him.

"Almost there," he said, mostly to encourage her.

"Almost where?" she asked with genuine interest this time.

"Going tree tapping. The first syrup of the season is always the sweetest."

"Why are you bringing me along for this?"

"To make a point."

"Can't you just tell me your point?"

And that might be the perfect encapsulation of their relationship thus far. He smiled and kept walking until he found the tree he'd come to see.

"There she is." Twenty feet tall. Thick enough around that he couldn't get both arms around it. It leaned slightly and the canopy of naked branches had provided enough shelter to the ground that almost all the snow had melted around it. "Beauty, isn't she?"

Fiona let her gaze travel all the way up the bark and back down again. "What's so special about this tree?"

That she'd clued in enough to use the word *special* warmed him up dangerously fast. It was special. Very much so, and he wanted her to get that. "My great-grandfather planted this tree when he was a boy. Among these evergreens."

"Come on, really?" She glanced at it again but with new appreciation that looked nice on her.

"Yep. And then when it grew, my grandma helped him tap it, and then my parents, and now me."

Setting down his bucket, he pulled the handheld drill bit from it and scouted for a good spot to put the hole. Gently, he pierced the bark, careful to drill at an angle so the syrup could run downhill.

Fiona watched for a few seconds and then let her gaze drift to the horizon. "Wow, it is really pretty out here."

"You haven't even tasted the syrup yet." He drilled a few more centimeters, checking the bark to be sure he'd tapped a healthy spot. If the wood shavings came out dark, he'd have to shift a bit. But the bits were fresh and light brown, the perfect place. "This tree is special. It has the lightest, the most golden syrup. A tree like this takes years and years to grow."

That was the point, the one she'd wanted him to just tell her. But the lessons of the maples couldn't be verbalized so easily, nor could you substitute a bunch of words for the nearly spiritual experience of tapping a tree. Together.

He glanced up at her and with her cheeks slightly red from the cold, her attention firmly on him and her mouth closed for once, Fiona was breathtakingly beautiful. Maybe it was the backdrop of forest. But he didn't think so.

Scarcely able to tear his gaze from her, he reached for the spile and hammer, inserting the spile into the hole he'd drilled and tapping lightly. "We're going to hold it still, and... Don't worry, I'm not going to hurt it."

Her genuine smile slayed him. Probably a good thing she didn't wield that thing too often.

"Now," he continued brusquely and hit the spile a couple more times with light strokes so he didn't split the bark. "We're going to tap it in."

When he pulled the plug from the spile, she leaned over immediately. "Where's the syrup? I think our tree is broken. Do we have a broken tree?"

He laughed. Point about taking it slow not absorbed obviously, but she'd said "our tree," and that was a whole different point that he liked. When Fiona dropped her act and showed him what was real and true about her, that did funny things to his insides. "It's not a syrup faucet. See, that's my point. A bucket like this could take a couple of days to fill. Good things are worth waiting for."

The syrup gathered at the end of the tap and Fiona took off one glove to catch it on her fingertip, bringing it to her mouth.

"Sweet, huh?" he asked her but it was rhetorical. He already knew the answer, could see it in her expression.

"It's not bad."

"And we haven't even boiled it down yet." He hung the bucket to catch the dripping syrup and glanced over at her.

"You really love it out here, don't you?" she asked.

Interesting subject change. Of course the answer was yes, but the fact that she'd noticed, that was something else.

"Yeah." He stared at the tree instead of her,

because all the air in his lungs had gotten trapped and he needed a moment to get his breathing in order. Except…she was so close, and so pretty. "I love being part of a tradition. Like my recipes. A lot of those are handed down over generations. Some people keep photo albums. I have this cookbook I keep by the stove that's full of recipes. And then, when I make something my grandma made, it helps me remember her. It's like she's almost there. Does that make any sense?"

He was rambling, saying things he'd never told anyone before. Sure, people could probably guess all of this about him, especially since the cookbook wasn't hidden. But it felt like a big thing to be confessing all of this on the heels of doing something so special together as tapping his great-grandfather's tree.

"Yeah," she said softly, her hand lightly resting on the tree truck as she spoke. "I get the remembering part. But for me sometimes remembering can be hard."

It was the most genuine bit of Fiona she'd shared and he wanted to understand her better. "What do you mean?"

"Let's just say, some memories are like syrup. They stick."

"But hopefully sweet." That seemed as good a time as any for the lesson to be over. Otherwise, he was going to kiss her again, and his ego hadn't been knit back together yet from the first blow it had received on that front. He picked up the supplies. "All right. Say goodbye."

Dutifully, Fiona patted the trunk. "Goodbye, tree."

They walked back to the truck in an unexpectedly comfortable silence. It was nice. Companionable. She didn't try to outsprint him and they stayed abreast the entire time. When they reached her door, she glanced up at him, blinking her gorgeous brown eyes.

"Listen, I think maybe we got off on the wrong foot," she said. "I'm sorry. It's just between my career and issues with my dad, this whole thing with Nate. I've been under a lot of stress."

She followed him as he set the supplies in the bed of the truck, so he turned to her. "I get it. I do. If you don't mind me asking, why'd you and Nate break up?"

Her shoulders slumped a little. "Something about being tired of trying to fit into my juggling act."

"Thought so." Nate was a loser who couldn't figure out how to handle a woman like Fiona. Obviously. Better for Derek though. "You know, if you really wanted to get Nate's attention, just slow down. Smell the maple syrup."

She laughed. "How about don't ever say that again."

But she said it without malice and things were sparking between them so nicely that he couldn't help but add, "I have just the event for that."

She looked intrigued and he jerked his head toward the truck, trundling her along to what wasn't a real date, but sure felt like the inevitable conclusion of whatever had been started underneath his family's tree. One thing he knew for sure, there was nothing artificial about the way he'd started to feel about Fiona.

The little town near the inn had a quaintness that Angela appreciated. What she did not appreciate was the tension filling the Jeep being driven by one very strong, silent type named Brandon Rangely.

"Your father is really excited about the blogger's dinner," she offered as he pulled into a spot at the end of the street and threw the vehicle into Park. "I'm happy to help pass out flyers."

Harris had rounded up the two of them about thirty minutes ago and begged them to head into town to get the word out about the big dinner his head chef would be preparing later in the week. Of course the bloggers and food critics who would be in attendance had the most sway when it came to the event, but it wouldn't do to have an empty dining room as they evaluated Derek's menu.

Brandon sat in the driver's seat for a minute, his jaw clenched. What was with him? He hadn't spoken two words to her since she'd accidentally fallen against him at the beanbag toss the day before. Honestly, she'd thought that would have been a tension breaker, but no.

"You didn't have to say yes," he finally said. "Advertising is my job."

Is that what was sticking in his craw? That Harris had suggested something that he considered his territory? "I thought the inn was a family business? Can't other people make suggestions?"

"It's not that." Brandon blew out a breath, still not looking at her in favor of staring out at the row of picturesque shops lining the main street in town. People strolled along the sidewalk dressed in coats and hats, smiling at antiques in windows and pointing at the old-fashioned ice cream parlor sign hanging long ways down the side of one building.

She'd like to be one of those couples, hand resting in the crook of Brandon's elbow. She didn't dare move. He had that bristly vibe about him as if he had something weighing on his mind but couldn't bring himself to blurt it out. Poor man. Didn't he know she had a degree that said she'd get it out of him one way or another? Lacing her fingers loosely over her stomach, she leaned her back against the Jeep's passenger door, opening up her body language. The message was clear: *I'm safe and available to talk to.*

Sneaking a glance at her from the corner of his eyes, he scowled. "You really don't see it."

"See what?"

"They're throwing us together with this made-up errand to hand out flyers."

She hid a smile. That had occurred to her. Clearly, he wasn't so keen on the idea of being fixed up, which she got. But well-meaning relatives aside…what was she supposed to do, pretend she had no interest in Brandon, solely because someone had orchestrated alone time with him? That wasn't happening. She had a unique opportunity here with the cozy confines and the romance of Vermont as a whole that she had no intention of blowing.

"I don't think there's some evil plan to force us together. I really just think your dad and Delia want the inn to be a success. The dinner is a huge part of that." She risked putting a hand on his arm. "Besides. Is it so terrible to spend an hour with me handing out flyers?"

His gaze landed on her hand and then cut up to her face. The tension got a lot thicker in a snap as something she couldn't interpret flashed through his expression. "Maybe not terrible. As long as no one gives you any snow cones."

She laughed at his deliberate joke. He never let that one rest, and for the first time, she wondered if it was because he felt a shared kinship to their past, as opposed to still thinking of her as his sister's annoying friend. "Here's an idea for you. Let's pretend that it doesn't matter if your dad is trying to throw us together, because we're adults who can manage our own lives, and we're capable of ignoring any external pressure. We can just pass out flyers, like he asked. If we have fun doing it, then that's a bonus."

He nodded slowly. "Okay."

"Also," she said, her voice dropping lower. "You should keep in mind that sometimes being thrown together with someone is an opportunity to get to know them better."

Somehow, that seemed to have done the trick,

or at least partially. The tension in his jaw eased off. Bristly vibe—fading. Looking decidedly intrigued by her point, he cocked his head. "I expected you to be a little bit more irritated at my father's meddling. You have a right to be miffed."

"Why would I be mad?" *I'm exactly where I want to be.* "He means well. And I make the best of any situation, unexpected or otherwise."

He eased around in his seat to face her more fully, a giant concession that had her crowing on the inside. Things were shifting between them, slowly but surely. She had boundless patience—after all, she'd been waiting him out for years.

"You seem...different than I remember," he said. "Less of a pain."

She laughed at what passed as a compliment in Brandon's world. "Because I'm not ten any longer?"

"Maybe." The look in his eye told her that he'd noticed she'd grown up all right and didn't hate the concept. "And because you have this way about you. You really listen. People don't do that very often, even here in Vermont where you know your neighbors. It's friendly, but almost like it's expected that you say hi, how are you? You know what I mean, right? People don't do it because they care about the answer. No one but my father and Delia seem to have a genuine interest in what I have to say, and for them, only when I talk about advertising for the inn."

"I'm interested," she said instantly. She couldn't

stress that enough. "I've always cared what you have to say."

"Always?"

She let their gazes lock and didn't back away from laying it on the line. "Maybe not always. But for a long time. I've been waiting for you to notice my, um…listening skills."

Brandon's jaw unclenched and he smiled, which was a little like the sun coming out from behind the clouds except a lot brighter and warmer. "Then I think we should hand out flyers like we said we would and make sure we have fun as a bonus."

That worked for her on so many levels. "You're on."

"Have dinner with me tonight," he threw in so casually that she did a double take to be sure she'd heard him correctly. Nothing but sincerity radiated back at her, and she was so shocked, she almost recoiled.

But caught herself at the last minute. "I wouldn't dare miss that."

With the anticipation of an honest date on the horizon, she let him help her out of the Jeep, quite unable to keep a secret grin off her face. Bonus points all around.

TEN

After a stop at the inn so Fiona could change and Derek could do a few things required for dinner that night, she found herself back in a moving vehicle next to the inn's head chef.

She couldn't stop sneaking glances at his profile. That maple syrup tapping thing? There'd been something magical about the woods and he'd been so different with her out there. More relaxed and just playing the part of himself, not her pretend boyfriend. Not one time had he smirked at her.

Honestly, it had been…not fun, exactly, because roller coasters were fun. Learning about Derek's history had been meaningful and deep, and somewhat like the syrup in the tree. Hidden beneath the surface of the rough exterior, but with right circumstances, the inner goodness made an appearance. She couldn't stop thinking about the taste she'd gotten of both the syrup and the man.

Derek drove them to the center of town. As they strolled along the main thoroughfare, she noticed that he had indeed gotten her to slow down, as advertised. But she didn't mind. There was a different vibe here in the town that she liked, one that called to her. It invited her to take her time and really enjoy what was happening around her.

"What brings us here?" she asked.

"All in good time," he told her as he led her into Porter's General Store.

Oddly, the interior had been cleared out and set up similar to a restaurant with tables and chairs, but each surface held jars of syrup with long stir sticks and pencils atop pieces of printed paper. People sat at each table engaged in conversation. Where were the rows of shelves and items for sale?

"What is all of this about?" she asked Derek.

"A maple syrup tasting. Think of it like wine tasting but with syrup."

Oh, man. Everything was about maple in Vermont. It was like the state bird had been replaced with a ewer and filled with tree sap. "Is this payback for the pancake-eating competition?"

"That's right." He grinned, but then his eyebrows went up as he caught sight of something over her shoulder. "Incoming. Stay in character."

He pulled Fiona in to his side and looped an arm around her as Nate and Hailey walked into the general store. *Oh, no.* She was so not ready to face them again. It had been nice to forget about all that for a few minutes.

Back to fake. It didn't feel so nice to be in Derek's embrace all at once, knowing it was for show.

What was wrong with her? Of course it was for show. She had a plan to get Nate's attention and Derek had agreed to help. That was all there was to it and wishing he'd touch her for real—because he wanted to—wasn't a thing.

Nate spread his hands as the couple approached, both wearing outdoor gear. Did the woman *own* a jacket in another color besides pink? This one was the color of cotton candy. If Fiona wore that, it would have stains all over it in five minutes.

"We meet again," Nate said, his voice clearly betraying the fact that it wasn't necessarily a happy coincidence.

Smooth as silk, Derek asked, "What have you two been up to today?"

"Well," Hailey said with an adoring glance at Nate that Fiona would bet she'd never had to practice. "We went to a yoga class, tried out snowshoeing and then we found this great little antique shop. What about you guys?"

That was the most boring day ever. And *yoga*? What in the world was that all about? Fiona's day had included a private lesson in tree tapping but she didn't want to share that all at once. It had nothing to do with Nate and Hailey.

"Well," she hedged, scrambling for something to say that wasn't the truth but wasn't precisely a lie either. "We… had a really busy morning planned, but we uh…"

Derek's hand stroked down her side and somehow her head ended up buried in his shoulder and wow, did it feel the opposite of forced to be snuggled up with this man. She lost her train of thought and wonder of wonders, her syrup tapper picked up the thread as if they'd planned out their response ahead of time.

"We ended up talking," he said but he was looking at Fiona, a hint of sparkle in his eye. "For hours and hours."

"Yeah. Hours." She had a feeling they were both remembering the conversation around the tree. It had been a really special time of connection and not just between the two of them. She'd felt his roots in the tree, a really weird kind of mystical deal that she'd have laughed off if someone had tried to describe it to her.

But it was as real as the man currently holding her.

"Well," Hailey returned brightly and gestured to the store at large. "I thought Nate had to try this. Syrup tasting was one of my favorite events growing up."

"My wine tasting palette is first-rate." Nate threw an apologetic glance at Hailey. "But…syrup? I think I'll sit this one out."

"Aww. Come on." Derek cuffed him on the shoulder with the back of his hand. "What are you afraid of? It'll be a blast."

"Actually, Hailey," Nate said, one finger in the air in the classic wait-a-minute position. "It's on."

"Great," Fiona said enthusiastically at the same time Derek did. Time for a little redemption in the contest arena because there was no way Derek didn't have this locked seven ways to Sunday.

"Have fun," Derek called after them as they made their way to their own table. No one suggested sitting together and Fiona wasn't sad. She wanted Derek and his expertise to herself, not sharing with anyone.

Everyone's coats came off and they put on their game faces simultaneously. Fiona leaned in and murmured to Derek, "Yoga? He doesn't do yoga. She's really pretty, though."

So apparently that had been bothering her. What had possessed her to confess that to Derek, of all people?

"Eh," Derek said with a shrug. "She's okay."

Fiona's heart fluttered a little. There was no reason for Derek to say that, but she had every suspicion he'd done so to make her feel better and that mattered. *That's* why she'd told him, why she'd had no trouble thinking of him as a confidant. A monumental piece of their relationship had changed. Or maybe they'd really formed a connection from the beginning, and that was what had made all this pretense seem so genuine.

The mayor grabbed a microphone and started the syrup tasting spiel. Apparently he emceed all the contests in town. "Folks, you've got five samples in front of you. As you try each one, fill out the card with your guess. And we'll see who really knows their syrup."

The crowd buzzed as they started on their individual jars of sticky sweet goodness.

"Okay." Derek shoved the first jar toward her. "Drink up."

"Are you serious? Come on. You want me to find the perfect brownstone in Brooklyn, I'm your girl. But this?" The whole concept was right up his alley and she'd expected him to do the honors.

"It's just like wine tasting," Derek insisted.

"It's maple syrup," she insisted right back. Duh. It tasted like syrup. No extra thought required. She didn't have any particular discernment when it came to tree sap.

"Yeah, *but*. What we call maple is really a combination of a hundred different sugars and amino acids." Derek smiled and suddenly, she couldn't take her eyes off his face. "They all combine differently, depending on how that particular tree woke up from winter."

He talked with his hands as he described a fascinating undertone to syrup, something she'd never looked at twice. This tasting event was an extension of their tree-tapping bond, another glimpse of what was inside him that he'd opted to share with her. It was a little overwhelming how easily this affected her.

"You're the expert then, Tree Man." She noted his irises had picked up the blue from his pullover, turning the most fascinating shade. The light in the general store showcased them perfectly. And she wanted to study them some more, not think about syrup. "You do the tasting."

"Close your eyes," he instructed.

"I don't want to close my eyes." As if. Then she'd miss out on the interesting things going on between his lashes. Oh, and she couldn't see Nate then either. Probably Nate should be more of a focus. "I want to see what they're doing."

Nate and Hailey were reading over the card and pointing at the jars. Fiona and Derek hadn't even glanced at theirs.

"Forget about Nate for a second and just clear your mind for once in your life." His smooth voice swept over her with all of these interesting notes, and Nate completely lost her attention. "Is your mind clear?"

"No, because you're still talking to me," she whispered hotly. How was she supposed to think about nothing when he was being this charming? She could feel his eyes on her and it was making her...*bothered* or something.

"Shut your eyes," he murmured, and goodness, she couldn't help but go along. "Give me your hand."

Before she could protest, he took her by the wrist, his fingers curling against her sweater sleeve, but the flimsy barrier of fabric was no match for the man's heat. A shock of awareness jolted through her. She was glad her eyes were closed so she could process it without cluing him in that this might be the most romantic scene she'd been in for quite some time.

The cool jar grazed her fingertips as he pushed it into her hand. "If this was wine, what would you do?"

"Drink it," she said automatically and then shrugged. "If this was wine, I would swirl it around."

"Right."

She accompanied that with the motion. A hint of sweetness drifted from the jar and *oh*. There was something there other than maple. She stirred the syrup with one of the tasting sticks to generate more of the scents.

"Check for unique tones," Derek encouraged.

"Seems smooth." She extracted one of the tasting sticks and placed it on her tongue. "Hmm. Kind of a hint of vanilla."

That had been unexpected. All of this was unexpected. And so much deeper than it had appeared on the surface.

"Yeah. Exactly." When her eyes blinked open, he was smiling at her proudly. "Depending on how the sap is heated, it brings out different vanillin in the flavor. Okay. Try this one."

He slid a different jar across the table and she tried not to be disappointed he hadn't taken her hand again.

"What about this one? What about the color?" He picked it up for her consideration and she immediately noticed the contents were a different color than the first one.

"I think I remember you saying the later in the season, the darker the color." That conversation had happened on the way back to the inn from the forest earlier. The man knew his tree sap. The shocking thing might be that she'd not only listened, she'd retained it.

A grin split his face, clearly showing that he was pleased she'd remembered. "That's right. So we'll mark it late season. You know, you're better at this than you thought."

The compliment warmed her thoroughly. Because it was genuine and completely unsolicited. "Thanks."

"And I would call that—" Derek pointed with his pencil in the direction of Nate. "A tell."

She glanced over out of the corner of her eye, and lo and behold, caught Nate staring at them as he completely ignored Hailey. He blinked and cut his gaze back to the table, murmuring something to his new girlfriend, all while still not looking at her.

The victory felt a little…hollow.

What was wrong with her? This plan had worked perfectly. They just needed to keep it up a little while longer and everything would come together before the end of the week. She could go back to New York with Nate ready to resume their relationship as if nothing had happened.

But something had happened. More than she'd taken the time to contemplate. He'd dumped her and moved on. Maybe getting him back wasn't her goal any longer. But what was?

She didn't find her answer in the bottom of any of the jars of syrup. They finished up their card, turned it in and had the pleasure of hearing their names called as the winners.

The mayor met them on the sidewalk outside the general store with a handshake. "Not bad for a newcomer. Don't forget your prize. Two tickets to Tuesday's MapleDance."

"Thanks!" Fiona accepted the bright red printed cardstock from the mayor, who nodded and took his leave. To Derek, she said, "I cannot believe we won. Five for five."

Nate and Hailey exited the store. Derek watched them approach and lifted his brows. "Hey, no hard feelings, Nate?"

"No," Nate insisted, though his face had this weird expression on it. "Not at all. Well. We'll see you guys back at the inn. We're off for a sunset stroll."

Nate pulled Hailey against his side and slung a possessive arm around her waist. Fiona took that as an opportunity to do the same with Derek. At one time, being this close to him would have put her back up. Now it just felt natural to touch him, a casual hand on his arm or shoulder. Strictly for show, of course. They were falling into their roles with ease.

Except it was more than that. She didn't hesitate to put a hand on his arm because they'd grown closer, thanks to his foresight in including her in something like tree tapping, which had nothing to do with Nate.

She owed Derek, if nothing else. He'd been an amazing fake boyfriend so far.

When Nate and Hailey were out of earshot, she rolled her eyes. "A sunset stroll. Someone's getting competitive."

"See? What did I tell you? I'd say he's intrigued by Vermont Fiona."

Honestly, Derek had more to do with that than Vermont. The man did have a way of getting her to slow down, and she didn't hate it. Didn't hate the way he looked at her sometimes.

"I think we're making progress," he said, his gaze on her with that little hint of warmth that she was coming to appreciate. "You want to make him jealous, right?"

"Yeah, seething." That much, she knew, and appreciated the reminder of what the stakes were here. There was no point to any of this if Nate didn't get a little taste of what he'd given up. Maybe that was enough for now. The rest, she'd figure out later.

"I'm training a new sous chef on tonight's dinner. Would Vermont Fiona like to join me for dinner for two?"

Extend their virtually perfect day with even more time together? He didn't have to ask her twice. "Vermont Fiona would love that. There is one thing I have to do first, though."

Corner an old man in his barn and sweet-talk him until he agreed to sell that field. Derek deserved that and so much more for this week. He didn't have to go to all this extra effort, but he had, and come through with flying colors. It was her turn to shine.

"Mr. Chauncey!" Fiona called out as she trod up the snow-covered hill to his barn, where he stood outside it watching her, both of his gloved hands on the barbed wire stretching between two posts. One stiff breeze might knock the whole contraption down, but he stubbornly clung to the wire as he wrangled it higher against the withered wood.

As metaphors went, that couldn't be clearer. He looked like he'd rather wrap the barbed wire around her neck than have a chat, but she didn't let it discourage her.

"Well, if good fences make good neighbors, I'd say we've got a long way to go." She smiled. Chauncey just stared at her as if she'd lost her mind. "Right. I was just hoping we could talk a little more privately."

"How about you get to the point? I got hungry sheep waiting."

That wasn't a no. "I wanted to discuss my client's offer to buy your field."

He chuckled and fed more wire around the second pole, but it really didn't look any sturdier than it had before he'd started. "Never gonna happen."

"You're growing weeds," she said with a confused shrug. "I've asked around town and this field has been sitting here for a while on the market. It's a solid offer. Why not sell it to Derek?"

"Because he's attracting the wrong element," Chauncey explained with a side eye for Fiona, as if he saw a woman with a couple of prison tattoos and a rap sheet instead of a successful real estate broker.

"What with his fancy cooking and turnip tartines or whatever they are. You and your type are changing this valley—and not for the better."

"Me? Sir, you have me pegged all wrong."

He lifted his brows as if to say *not likely*. "Your fancy scarf is snagged on the fence post."

She glanced down to see a length of barbed wire poking through her favorite blue Hermes from Barney's. That was an even more appropriate metaphor. Vermont was systematically destroying everything she'd brought with her from New York: her skillset, her clothes. Her ability to speed through a sale, a conversation, an activity.

No—this stubborn old man was not going to break her. Derek needed his fresh vegetables. She could easily picture him out in this field as he tended the rows with his careful, methodical touch. The same touch that made her shiver when he cupped her elbow as if to promise he could tend to her just as thoroughly.

And just maybe she wanted to be successful in getting Derek this field for more reasons than because they had a deal.

ELEVEN

When she came downstairs for dinner that evening in a blue sleeveless dress and heels, Fiona ran into her father in the lobby.

"Wow, you look beautiful, honey," Harris said.

"Thanks, Dad."

He crossed his arms and she got the impression that had been a lead-in to what he really wanted to discuss. "So tell me, what is this charade with Derek?"

Oh, that. Was this the part where he planned to go all parental on her and demand that Derek do right by his daughter? Well, she didn't fully know what the deal was with the charade. And didn't need her father reminding her that she'd been looking forward to dinner more than she should have when everything about it was supposed to be fake. "Are there no secrets in the state of Vermont?"

"Come on, if it impacts the inn, it's my business."

Of course. Silly of her to think maybe he'd been concerned that Fiona was falling into something that was destined to be a problem later down the road when she couldn't sort out the real from pretend. Instead, his interest started and ended with his precious inn.

Her father shrugged. "We've got those food bloggers coming in in a couple of days and Derek has to be focused. Future of the inn could be at stake."

"I know. Of course. The *inn*," she stressed.

His face closed in as he caught the disappointment in her tone. "I've got a raccoon situation down at the carriage house."

Sure. Bail like always, Dad.

Angela came down the stairs wearing a snazzy black dress as Fiona's father shrugged on his coat.

"Hey," Ang called. "Ready to eat?"

"Dad, do you want to join us?" Now why had she gone and done a thing like that? Well, no mystery really. She'd been beating her head against this wall so long that it felt normal to advertise her desperate need to get some kind of emotional reaction from her dad.

"No, that's okay. You lovely ladies have a nice dinner."

And that was how it was done, folks. Fiona should take a lesson in how to take the emotion out of a situation and apply that to every second she spent with Derek. None of the closeness they'd shared today had been real, and this was the perfect opportunity to reset herself before show time.

"What was that all about?" Ang asked, ever the psychologist. She picked up on things normal people didn't.

"Ancient history."

"You and your dad really need to have a heart to heart."

"You think I haven't tried?" Fiona was *not* the problem here. "He has this amazing gift for changing the subject. Speaking of... How was your day?"

Ang grimaced and let her off the hook. "Oh, it was great. Your father had Brandon and I handing out flyers for the bloggers' dinner all over town."

"He put you to work? Ang, you're supposed to be on vacation. I'm sorry. I'll have a word with him."

"No!" Ang's manicured hands flew up in protest. "Don't you dare. It was fine."

Delia bounded up and took Ang by the arm. "Ladies, there's been a slight change in the seating arrangement tonight. Angela, you're going to be right over there by the fireplace."

Following the line of Delia's nod, Ang brightened when she saw Brandon sitting at a table for two. Geez. Were the two of them finally getting somewhere?

"Oh, I like this," Ang murmured.

Brandon waved and popped to his feet, coming over to escort Ang to the table. "If Fiona gets to mock date, maybe we can as well."

Judging by the look on Ang's face as she drank in Brandon wearing a sport coat and tie, there wasn't a whole lot of "mock" happening here. They headed off without acknowledging Fiona once. Fine by her.

"Fiona, your date is waiting." Delia showed her to the other dining room where Derek sat at a cozy table.

He glanced up and the other diners ceased to exist.

The world ceased to exist. Air didn't seem to be a thing either, not when she had Perfection as a dining companion. He'd donned a blue suit jacket that put that snap and sizzle in his silvery-blue irises, and when he saw her, he unfolded from his seat in slow motion, spilling his presence into the room.

"Good evening." He pulled back her chair and waited for her to sit, then pushed it in.

"Hi," she said breathlessly. "Oh, no duck boots tonight?"

Smooth, girl. She might as well have a sign on her forehead that said, *Don't mind me, I have first date jitters.*

Except this wasn't a date.

Derek laughed. "My loafers turn into duck boots at midnight."

See? He knew it wasn't a date. They were playing a part filled with some fairy dust and good luck, but eventually, everything would turn back to normal. The problem was that Fiona still couldn't wrap her head around why that didn't seem so great.

Angela followed Brandon to the table and waited as he pulled back her chair, then took her seat. Like a true gentleman, he pushed her chair in. His thumb brushed across her bare back and her breath caught at the contact. It had been an accident—probably—but no less affecting.

More bonus points.

"So," she said huskily as Brandon slid into his own chair. "We're mock dating?"

He might have blushed a little. Or else it was a reflection of the merry fire crackling in the fireplace next to their table. He'd picked one tucked away in the smaller dining room where the tables only sat two.

The date-night room, as Angela thought of it. Romance dripped from the chandelier and bled from the fabric-covered walls.

"I didn't want to answer any uncomfortable questions, so I made that up," he confessed. "I'd rather have dinner without catering to anyone else's curiosity, just in case that flyer scenario earlier *was* a plot to match us up."

She held out her wine glass so Brandon could fill it from the uncorked bottle of white chilling by the table. "Can't have anyone thinking they put one over on us."

"No way," he agreed and poured his own wine.

"If we decide to date for real, it'll be because we figured out all on our own that we're both good looking, successful people with interesting things in common."

"Exactly." Brandon's brows came together. "I mean…what? You think I'm good looking?"

She rolled her eyes. "Duh. It's kind of a fact. Tall. Blond. Great shoulders. I'm not blind."

The waiter picked that inopportune moment to approach their table to recite the specials. Brandon's gaze strayed to his menu and back to Angela when he must have thought she wasn't paying attention, but she always paid attention when it counted. After they ordered, she decided to give him a break. She'd opened the door. Brandon needed to walk through it of his own accord, not because she'd pressured him.

Of course, he *had* been the one to suggest dinner. Maybe she just needed to lay low and let things play out naturally.

"Forget all of that for now," she said. "Tell me what other things you're working on to promote the inn. Your father said something about a website update?"

Brandon visibly relaxed. "I've added a reservation portal. It's really slick. When customers can book online, Dad doesn't have to pay a sourcing fee to travel websites, so it's a win-win. I just finished testing it."

Impressed, she clinked her glass to his. Nothing captivated her more than a smart man who solved problems with flair and style. "That's great. You did it all yourself?"

He nodded. "I've always dabbled in that sort of thing, even when I worked in New York. I like designing websites. It's a puzzle that just needs me to put the pieces in the right order."

"That's what I like about psychology," she said with a smile. "Told you we have things in common."

His gaze sharpened as he evaluated her. "I wasn't going to disagree. I'm curious about something then. We have some stray pieces floating around here that

I'm having trouble deciding where they fit. Help me out."

She shivered as his voice lowered. They had definitely moved on to more personal talk. "Sure. What's the first piece?"

"You're my sister's friend. How does that fit into the big picture?"

"Well," she drawled, recognizing that he was asking a much more delicate question than it would seem at first glance. He meant if they were romantically involved. That he was even thinking in that direction excited her. "If you're worried about how she might react if she found out we were doing more than mock dating, I would say don't worry. We're tight. Always will be. If something happens between you and me that maybe strains that friendship, then we'll deal with it. I would like to think that Fiona and I can weather anything. Does that answer your question?"

He sipped his wine as if contemplating. "It's getting there."

That sounded so promising she had to throw in, "Of course, I can't predict the future. There's really only one way to find out what temperature the water is. Dive in."

"I'm more of a wader." Brandon quirked his lips into a smile. "But I'm not opposed to getting my feet wet."

Message received. He was a take-it-slow kind of guy. That was fine with her. As long as he wasn't avoiding the water entirely, she could work with that.

She raised her wine glass. "Here's to finding the right spot for all the puzzle pieces."

Derek took his seat, thrilled his tongue still worked. Fiona looked amazing in a pretty blue sleeveless dress, but the best part was her smile. She'd finally relaxed around him, seeming not to even notice that Nate and Hailey had just walked into the dining room.

Nate sure noticed Fiona, his eyes nearly popping out of his head as he stared at them from his peripheral vision. Derek didn't bother to acknowledge the Loser.

"Fair warning," he said to Fiona. "I may have to duck back into the kitchen occasionally to be sure my sous chef has everything running smoothly."

Fiona clued in that the object of her affection had arrived and glanced over at Nate and Hailey, her expression darkening. That was enough to put Derek in a reckless mood.

"Did you just hear a can opener?" he asked.

Though that had probably not been the best question to ask in a dining room full of inn guests who were about to be eating dishes from his kitchen that he did not prepare. While he had some qualms, he did not hire incompetent people. Mica, his sous chef, had this locked.

"If we're playing the happy couple," Fiona

singsonged under her breath, "you should pay attention to me, not your kitchen."

"Okay. Well then, you have to look at me as well."

Her gaze was on him, not Loser. Success all the way around. Probably he shouldn't examine how out of control his ego got whenever Nate entered the equation. There was just something about that guy that chafed him the wrong way, and the fact that he couldn't see how amazing and bright and funny Fiona was... He didn't deserve her.

She chuckled. "All right. Well, I guess this little *fake* relationship of ours could use a little give and take."

Timely reminder. She wasn't sitting at this table because Derek had asked her on a date and she'd said yes. They were playing a part. Period. Wishing she could see him for his good qualities instead of strictly as a mechanism to pull off her agenda didn't help matters.

He hadn't realized just how much he would hate it. How his own part in this would start to feel real, and how difficult of a position that put him in.

"Okay," he agreed readily and unfolded his napkin, placing it over his thigh. "Let's just do our best."

"Oh, just admit it." She draped her own napkin over her lap. "You love being a chef because then you get to torture everyone with your perfectionism."

He couldn't let that go. "Is that what you think?" Her gaze flew to his and stuck. "The best dishes of my life... My grandma's wedding meatballs. My dad's shepherd's pie. Maple torte on my aunt's birthday. To me, food isn't about perfection. It's about love…and family…and tradition."

He swallowed and picked up the bottle of wine chilling in a silver bucket at the side of the table. As he poured, he glanced at her because she had yet to speak. She was gazing at him with this expression on her face he couldn't decipher. Maybe he didn't want to. She probably thought he was nuts to go off on such a rant about a thing like cooking.

People seldom understood or cared about old fashioned values, the same ones that made him tick. That filled his heart. Fiona Rangely was no different.

He just sometimes wished that she was. A dangerous place to be. They were only sitting here eating together because her ex had spaghetti instead of a brain, and as soon as he figured out that letting Fiona go had been a mistake, Derek's role would be over.

None too soon. He should untangle himself from her as soon as possible before it was too late. The last thing he needed was another broken heart because he'd fallen for something that wasn't real.

"Anyway," he continued. "I'd say by the look on Nate's face our plan is going rather well. How are things on your end?"

"I tracked down Chauncey today. He is one tough nut."

Chuckling, he lifted his wine glass to his mouth to sample the Chardonnay. Nice. Sweet. Hint of green apple. "Tell me about it."

"Well, don't worry, I'm tougher. I actually have a mission planned for tomorrow. You in?"

No. He should say no. "Sure."

Okay, he had to admit he was curious what she might have up her sleeve that could possibly change Chauncey's mind, because he'd tried everything else. And he wanted that field.

He was coming to want this charade to be over even more than he wanted the field.

Lifting his glass toward her, he said, "Here's to solving all our problems."

They clinked glasses and in the silence, he heard Hailey's voice as she spoke to Nate. He wasn't eavesdropping per se; she had a very high voice that carried.

"So I told Robin if her brother was going to act like that... Nate, are you listening?"

No, he was staring at Fiona, and he was dumb enough to admit it to his girlfriend. "Yeah, I just think it's odd Fiona didn't bring her cell phone to dinner. That's a first."

Derek hid a smile. He hadn't even seen her cell phone today, mostly—he assumed—because she still couldn't get a signal, but Loser didn't have to know that. Let him think that Fiona had abandoned her cell phone addiction in favor of spending real quality time with her new boyfriend. It was good for Nate to understand that while he didn't appreciate Fiona, other people did.

Hailey put her fork down. "Nate, what's come over you?"

"What?" he asked.

Poor clueless man. Derek actually felt sorry for him. And he'd spent way too much time worrying about a guy who'd screwed up with Fiona and was currently screwing up with his new girlfriend.

Derek was having dinner with the prettiest woman in the room and he wasn't a screw-up. "So," he said to her. "What's the deal with you and your dad? That's the one answer the staff rumor mill can't grind up."

"It's just..." She kept her gaze on her plate for a beat and then glanced up at him through her lashes, something soft and vulnerable flashing through her expression. "My mom passed away when I was twenty. My life was turned upside down."

Derek nodded gravely. "I'm sorry."

That must have been so tough. He still had his mom and managed to find new ways to be thankful for it every day.

"Yeah, you think I love the city? My mom loved it even more."

Her misty smile pulled one out of him as well. It was clear that she had many good memories of her mother and he didn't dare interrupt. This was a side of her he hadn't yet discovered. A side he liked.

"She lived life at a gallop, and well, I take after her." That widened his smile because of course she did. "We had this amazing apartment overlooking Central Park. It was the perfect location. In winter, we'd open the window and smell chestnuts roasting. We'd hear cars driving by all night. In summers, Mom and I would sit together and watch hansom cabs trotting by. Dad always thought it was so loud and busy, but Mom and I loved it."

"Sounds great." And he meant it too.

He had similar memories of living in Paris: the hustle of street vendors, the rumble of the Metro beneath his feet on the south side of the Seine where the tracks lay closer to the surface, the chattering of couples at the multitudes of sidewalk cafes.

New York City had become intertwined with the love she had for her mom. He got that. Just like Paris reminded him of Lizette and her treachery. He still couldn't see pictures of the Eiffel Tower without recalling that it had been in his peripheral vision as Lizette tearfully told him she had to break things off because her husband had caught on to her deception.

Talk about a blind side.

"Yeah, it really was great. After my mom passed away, my dad… He actually sold the apartment. With no warning. Sold it and moved up here and really put our past behind him. Things have been a little strained between me and my dad ever since."

That was not what he would have guessed lay at the root of the obviously strained relationship. His entire perception of Fiona shifted, wrenching something in his chest.

She loved and honored tradition as much—if not more—than he did.

New York held all her traditions, though, which may as well be as far from his Vermont lifestyle as the east lay from the west, but roots were roots. And he liked Fiona's. "That explains quite a bit."

It wasn't lost on him that she'd readily volunteered this information, as if they were a real couple on a date of discovery. It was humbling and surprising and he did not take these admissions lightly. Maybe things between them had passed into another stage for her as well.

"You have recipes to keep memories alive," she said. "For me, it's like a place. You know, the city is my tie to our past. To my mom. I'm like the last soldier of my family clinging to this island of Manhattan."

The forlorn note in her voice stuck in his heart. "All of that is a tough battle to fight on your own."

A resounding crash from the kitchen punctuated that statement and he flinched.

Fiona jerked her head toward the sound of chaos in his sanctuary. "I think they probably need you in there."

From this vantage point, he could see Mica's white chef's hat bobbing with the man's frenzied movements. No one's dinner had come out burned yet and broken dishes were easily swept up.

Whatever was unfolding at this table was more important. "You know what? It can wait."

Somehow, he had a feeling she understood what a huge concession he'd just made for her. For this evening he suddenly didn't want to end.

Surely it was okay to keep up appearances a while longer while they sorted through the unexpected closeness that had developed between them.

TWELVE

The next morning, the rooster crowed same as always, but Fiona was already out of bed, dressed and walking down the slope toward the lake when she heard him. She didn't have but a few more days in Vermont and there was something so…peaceful about the quiet snow in the morning. She was going to miss it.

The realization surprised her. Lots of things surprised her lately. Like how much she'd enjoyed dinner last night with Derek. He had this easy way about him that invited confidences. He had zero pretension and such a charming smile.

All at once, her morning walk got a whole lot more interesting as Nate emerged from the woods. Alone. Dressed for a jog, not yoga. She smiled as he ran toward her, his gaze firmly on her instead of the scenery.

"Hey, you," Nate said as he jerked to a halt.

"Hi."

"You might want to tighten those laces." Nate

pointed to her shoes. "I hit a patch of ice as I jogged past that last tree."

"Thanks, but I actually think I'm going to walk the rest of the way."

"You?" Nate pointed at her, his expression incredulous. "You are going to walk?"

"Yeah, sure." She shrugged.

"What, did you sprain an ankle or something?"

This was the conversation they were having? She'd expended enormous effort to throw her relationship with Derek in Nate's face and the first chance they got to speak alone, he wanted to discuss the stability of her ankles?

"No, it's just that I want to take in the scenery." Who wouldn't?

"You know, you seem different out here." He crossed his arms over his chest, eyeing her with confusion.

He seemed different too. Had he always been so short? Maybe the ground was uneven here by the lake or something. She could look him in the eye without straining. After spending so much time craning her neck to meet Derek's gaze, this seemed…weird.

"Chalk it up to Vermont." And then she opted to be honest with him. "I actually have been discovering a few things lately."

Like how much she enjoyed having a man pay attention to her. If Nate had wanted more of her time, why hadn't he orchestrated a way to do that? Derek would never put up with Fiona cancelling on him.

He'd find some way to come to her if she had to work, to create a fun date no matter what the circumstances.

"Yeah? I guess you have." He shifted from foot to foot, hesitating as if he had something to say and didn't know quite how to phrase it. "You know, I saw you and Derek at dinner last night. I hope you don't mind me asking. What do the two of you have in common?"

Almost nothing. But that didn't seem like such a big minus all at once. She and Nate were cut from the same cloth, loved the city, the busyness, the restaurants and theatre. Look how that had turned out. "Guess I get to discover that too. See you."

With that, she skirted him to continue on with her walk. That had been a great segue toward her ultimate goal. She had Nate hooked on the line. She might not have to do anything more than reel him in. The problem was that her fishing pole had switched ponds when she wasn't looking.

By the time Angela woke up the next morning after her delicious—in more ways than one—dinner with Brandon, Fiona had already left, likely to go for a jog. Honestly, running on purpose? It made Angela want to gag. But Fiona loved it.

Humming, Angela took a shower and got dressed. That was when she saw the handwritten note Fiona had left her on the antique bedside table, which was amusing. Handwritten—because Fiona's cell phone didn't work out here, so she'd had to resort to archaic, backwoods communication devices like pen and paper. The horror.

Hope dinner went well. Do me a favor and talk to Brandon this morning about helping me with a project. More details soon! —Fi

Subtle. Fiona had given Angela an excuse to seek out Brandon, and Angela just might kiss her for it later.

It didn't take long to find Fiona's brother. Brandon was outside chopping wood like a boss, and without an ounce of shame, she watched him swing the axe a few times.

Finally she had to interrupt him because she did have to secure his help according to Fiona's note. Bounding down the front steps, she crunched through the snow, halting a few feet away until he noticed her. He glanced up from his task, his expression decidedly warmer than it had been a few days ago when he caught sight of her.

"I'm here to recruit you," she told him. "Fiona told me about putting some sort of secret mission together."

"Oh." Brandon stacked a couple of logs in the wheelbarrow to his left, his attention on Ang and not the wood. One piece toppled off the back side, but he didn't even notice. "What is it?"

"Who knows?" Angela shrugged cheerfully and bent to pick up the errant log. "But you know Fiona has a way of shaking things up."

Like pushing her brother and friend together. Guess that answered Brandon's question from last night about how his sister might feel about it. She'd be nothing but encouraging if they decided to stop taking things so slowly. But while Angela respected Brandon's molasses approach, that didn't mean she had to be as cagey. There was no time like the present to see if they could fit a few more puzzle pieces into the scene.

"So," she drawled. "How is the whole moving back home thing going? Are you enjoying living up here?"

It was a loaded question and she didn't doubt he understood that. They couldn't date as easily if they lived in two different states. Sure they could make concessions, but this was getting to the heart of where their futures lay. And she wanted to envision this flirtation becoming something more.

"Yeah. For now." Brandon busied himself with a few more logs. "I wouldn't mind getting back into the action, but first I need to make sure Dad's inn is a success."

That scored Angela right across the heart. When had Fiona's brother developed such a sense of responsibility toward their father? That made her wonder if things with the business side of the inn were grimmer than Harris had let on or if Brandon might be using this as an excuse not to delve back into the tech world in New York City.

She knew a little about how he'd started his own dotcom company and how it had gone belly up due to bad timing and some manufacturing issues, about which Fiona had only supplied a few hazy details. Brandon had retreated to Vermont to lick his wounds and stuck around the inn once he realized his father had need of someone with his tech skills.

"You're such a nice guy," Ang told him as he lifted the handles of the wheelbarrow full of logs. "No wonder I always liked you."

Bam. That had just slipped out, but she wouldn't apologize for calling a spade a spade. Molasses had its place, but sometimes it benefited from a little heat to really get it going.

"You know," Ang murmured, moving in a little closer once his hands were good and occupied with the wheelbarrow. "When we were kids, I didn't chuck my snow cones at just anyone."

"Well, I only pulled the hair of girls I liked," Brandon returned.

Yes! Finally! This flirtation had come together into an intersection of freely admitted interest. Angela resisted the urge to pump her fist and/or whack him upside the head for taking so long to figure this out. What was it about romance that made people stupid?

"Do you want to take a break later and go into town?" she asked. "Maybe put up some more flyers and find a place that sells snow cones?"

He smiled. "You're on."

The long moment stretched as they both let it soak in that they'd crossed that imaginary line separating them. Fiona materialized from around the corner of the house and they jumped apart like guilty teenagers.

At some point they'd have to come clean to everyone, but for now, she liked having a romance brewing that still held a world of possibilities.

"Hey," Fiona called. "The mission is a go."

Angela tucked her hand into the crook of Brandon's elbow, suddenly thrilled that whatever Fiona had cooked up gave her an opportunity to spend more time with this man she'd somehow managed to knock out of his oblivion. She couldn't wait to see what happened.

Derek parked his ancient pickup truck just off the main drive to Chauncey's farm, Fiona, Brandon and Angela in tow. Fiona's plan for changing the old man's mind about selling his field to Derek was either brilliant or spectacularly foolish. Maybe both simultaneously, which frankly sounded like a pretty good description of his dealings with Fiona as a whole.

"How did I get roped into this again?" He hefted the first load of lumber from the truck bed.

Fiona patted his arm. "I had some inspiration. I didn't get to where I am by being timid."

No, he would never make the mistake of thinking that. Fiona resembled a bulldozer ninety percent of the time, which explained why he always felt flattened after five minutes in her presence. The real question was why he kept lining up for more.

Well, he knew that one. Because he'd begun to

hope their relationship had gained some legs. Real ones.

"Tell me what we're doing again," Angela asked as Derek set down the bucket and dry bagged concrete on the ground near the broken-down fence.

"Mending fences. Literally." Fiona grabbed the sagging barbed wire in emphasis. "And apparently cow sitting."

One of Chauncey's steers stood by the fence blinking big brown eyes at the interlopers. Someone, likely Chauncey, had tied him up to the gate, so they'd have to work around him.

"I want to show Chauncey that we can be good neighbors," Fiona continued. "He's plowing his south field right now so we probably have a couple of hours."

"Looks like we have our work cut out for us," Derek commented mildly, betraying nothing of his thoughts on the matter. Hard work didn't bother him. Fiona did though, in a not so bad way with her hair blowing in the breeze and a mischievous smile on her face.

"Let's get started!" Fiona and Angela swung open the gate so they could start pulling apart the hold the barbed wire had on the cracked fence posts.

Derek measured and sawed and poured concrete, while Brandon dug new holes and helped set the new fence posts. It didn't escape his notice that anytime Angela picked up a tool, Brandon moved right into her personal space, wrapping his arms around her to show her how to use it. She'd glance behind her, shooting Fiona's brother a smile laden with all kinds of meaning.

Apparently that was a thing, then. He wondered when that had bloomed, not that it was any of his business, but he liked Brandon. Had a healthy amount of respect for the man's marketing strategies. He deserved to be happy.

Since there was no audience to play for, he didn't do the same sort of moves with Fiona. But they still managed to wind up in the same place at the same time more often than not, like when he held a board so she could use the cordless screwdriver to fasten it to the new posts. What did it say about his mental state that he wished she'd shoot him secret smiles over her shoulder?

But it wasn't an unpleasant morning. He liked physical labor, and the fence ended up looking pretty good for a bunch of novices putting it together. He just couldn't get dinner last night out of his head. There had been a few moments when he'd swear that Fiona had forgotten all about Nate, and the two of them had connected on a deeper level.

He needed to forget about that. The whole point of their pretense was for Fiona to mend her own fences with Nate. If she couldn't see that Loser wasn't good enough for her that meant Derek couldn't tell her either. She had to figure it out on her own.

They stood back to admire their handiwork and he nodded. "Not bad."

"What is that noise?" Angela asked as a rumbling got louder and louder.

157

"Tractor," Derek said at the same time Fiona said, "He's coming back."

They scrambled for the truck, throwing tools and supplies into the bed and laughing as they fled the scene of the crime. When they got back to the inn, Brandon and Angela disappeared, both pretty much lost in each other.

He and Fiona strolled around the house toward the front door. Dare he hope she had as much reluctance as he did to end the afternoon? They'd worked well together. Seamlessly, in fact, often reading each other's minds as they put the pieces of the new fence in place.

"I'd love to see the look on Chauncey's face when he sees our work," Fiona commented.

"I got to hand it to you, you do think outside the box." Once the finished product was in place, his opinion leaned more toward the plan being brilliant. The fence had been falling down; now Chauncey didn't have to worry about it.

The fact that she'd give up her vacation time to do something like that for an old man who hadn't been very nice to her, strictly for Derek's benefit, choked him up a little.

"You have to, to succeed in my business." She stopped and glanced up at him. "Haven't you ever wanted more for yourself? A chef of your talents would be in high demand in New York."

The compliment sank into him with unexpected force. From anyone else, he'd brush off the sentiment, but Fiona didn't give that kind of praise easily. Plus, she must frequent restaurants of pretty high caliber on a regular basis—for her to tell him he had talent put him in a dangerous, hopeful place, like she might be seeing *him* instead of solely being focused on Nate. "I have everything I need right here."

"So, you're content with all this? Small town life forever?"

Where was she going with this? Fishing for whether he'd come visit her in New York later, maybe on a semi-permanent basis? If so, he needed to nip that idea in the bud as fast as possible.

"Growing up, I couldn't wait to get away. When I went to culinary school in Paris, I had an apartment overlooking the city, a French girlfriend, a different amazing restaurant every night." It all unfolded in his mind's eye, especially the part where he got disillusioned. That had happened on the heels of learning Lizette's secret. "Then one day, sitting on the banks of the Seine, I realized I missed home. This place just grows on you."

Fiona's gaze hadn't left his face and they were connecting again, like they had last night at dinner. And just like last night, it felt like their interactions were genuine. No audience. No false smiles or strategy. Just two people talking about their hopes and dreams and weaving threads that were harder and harder to pull apart.

He didn't want to pull them apart. He liked connecting with her, uncovering these surprising layers that he never would have noticed if they hadn't agreed to mock date this week. Except the fake part of this had started to fade. A date was a date whether she'd planned for it to be that way or not. He couldn't erase his feelings.

Before he could say anything, Nate crunched through the snow in dress shoes. He wore an expensive suit that marked him a city boy, and the contrast between him and Derek couldn't be clearer. Great. Derek nearly rolled his eyes at the unfortunate timing.

Or maybe given the circumstances, the timing had been perfect. Derek needed to reel it all back anyway. Fiona hadn't given him the slightest indication her goals had changed here. Mooning over her wouldn't change the fact that she'd had Nate in her sights from the first moment.

"What have you two been up to?" Nate asked. He asked things like that a lot, as if Derek and Fiona owed him a copy of their itinerary.

"Just doing a little work." Fiona laughed nervously. "Why are you so dressed up?"

"Oh, for the dance tonight," he said. "Last night of MapleFaire and all."

"Yeah, I better get cleaned up too," Derek said. "We're also going to the dance. Don't want to waste our free tickets."

And Derek couldn't find a shred of shame for throwing that back in Nate's face, reminding him they'd won the tickets at the syrup tasting.

"Don't you have to cover dinner?" Fiona asked, her interest genuine. Why, because she wanted to go to the dance? Surely she'd realized that he planned to take her.

"Nah. My sous chef can handle it." Wow, how many times had he said that lately? Too many. Or not enough since they were still faking this relationship for everyone, including themselves.

He slung an arm around her because he still could, though the time would come when she wouldn't welcome that kind of thing.

"Oh, letting go of control," Fiona said with a pleased note in her voice. "I like it."

Given the way she'd leaned right into his embrace, she liked that too, and it sat on his chest funny. The lines between pretense and reality had gotten so blurry he wondered if either of them knew where they were anymore.

"I better go check on him, just to be sure. Not a control thing," he threw in because of course that was what it looked like.

Better that than the truth, though. He wanted to ask Fiona if she'd gotten as tangled up in the lines as he had. He needed to leave before he found out the answer wasn't the one he hoped for.

THIRTEEN

D erek jetted off, leaving Fiona face to face with Nate, who looked great in his dark suit. For some reason, she couldn't find the energy to care. She'd spent the morning in pursuit of a man's dream—owning his own vegetable field—and that had meant something to her. To Derek.

A lot simmered beneath the surface of their relationship, things she'd been ignoring. But they'd come swimming to the forefront as she'd watched her "boyfriend" get his hands dirty doing something nice for his neighbor. Derek was so much more than just a chef. He had depth and a solid presence that spoke to her. He wouldn't be the kind of guy to dump a woman the second he felt a little pushed aside by her schedule. No, he'd muscle his way into her day one way or another, laughing about how she never smelled the roses so he was bringing them to her...

Or something like that. If this was a real relationship.

Nate had not only intruded on their conversation,

he'd introduced a level of reality that she wasn't terribly happy about, and it put her in a not so great mood. "I'd better go get ready, so... See you later."

"Yeah, okay. Hey, Fiona, I need to talk to you."

His brown eyes softened as he looked at her, so much like old times that she nearly got caught up in it. But then Hailey clicked down the stairs in her heels, dressed to the nines like Nate in her pink dress and yet another pink coat.

"Oh, hey." Nate put his arm around his girlfriend. "That was fast."

Hailey gave Fiona a pained smile. Obviously she'd caught the look Nate had given Fiona and hadn't been too thrilled. Well, honestly, Fiona didn't quite know how she felt about it, either. Nate and Hailey were together and it felt really bad and wrong all at once to be systematically pulling Nate away from this woman, who had entered into a relationship with him under completely above-board circumstances.

This was turning into a mess of the highest order.

The couple strolled away and Fiona went inside the inn. Her father met her in the lobby.

"Oh, honey," he called. "Can I have a word?"

Anything to distract her from the swirl of confusion in her head. "Sure, what's up, Dad?"

"I just got a phone call from Chauncey."

Wow, that was fast. "Oh, was he excited?'

"Not exactly. He's furious. You didn't by any chance rebuild his fence?"

"Wait. He's not happy?" And then it really sank in

that Chauncey had called her father to *complain* about getting a brand new fence *for free*. "What is *wrong* with this place?"

"People up here are proud and self-reliant. It's best not to burn any bridges. I was hoping someday you might want to spend more time up here. You do seem to be taking to this place."

Ugh, not this again, like he could magic away the fact that he'd sold her childhood and traded it for an inn that had none of her memories stored in it.

"Dad, don't forget. This whole Vermont thing is just an act." It was as much a reminder to her as it was to her father. Though it was a toss-up which of them needed it more.

"Right." He pointed to the ceiling. "I got a plumbing thing."

Delia crossed into the room, wearing such a sympathetic expression Fiona didn't have to ask if she'd overheard every word. "Are you and your dad ever going to really talk?"

"I'm not holding my breath." If Delia could see the issue lay with Harris, why didn't she just talk to him? She could tell him he was being stubborn, that he was the one avoiding their issues. Nothing Fiona had tried worked.

"Cinderella, you better hurry up," Delia said in a welcome subject change. "You have a dance to get to."

A long hot shower went a long way toward improving Fiona's mood. The fence thing still chafed at her, though. If that Hail Mary hadn't worked, how was she going to get Derek that field? Chauncey defied all her knowledge and experience on how to buy real estate. She had to come through for Derek, especially after he'd been so great at his part of the bargain.

A little too great. What would he say if he knew she'd gotten lost in the playacting—and more than once?

He'd laugh, no question. As he should. It was ridiculous to even think about Derek and herself as a couple outside of this deal they'd made. They had nothing in common, like Nate had said. So why was she still thinking about how it seemed like Derek knew exactly how to handle her tendency to hide from her emotions with busyness?

She had to get over herself.

"I wish I'd packed more evening wear options," she groused to Ang, who already looked beautiful in a mint green dress that set off her wild red curls.

"Okay," Ang said. "It's almost time."

The *chop-chop* was implied—for once. Ang had been telling Fiona to hurry up for fifteen minutes. But none of Fiona's dresses felt right. Derek was tall and brown-haired and rugged. He wouldn't go for sleek and sophisticated. She needed to look *real*.

"Come out," Ang instructed with the patience of a saint. Fiona had already changed four times and this was the very last dress she'd brought that could conceivably work for a formal dance.

She tiptoed out of the bathroom to the bedroom, where Ang stood by the bed waiting to evaluate round four. When her friend's face lit up, Fiona knew she'd found the one.

"Oh, Fiona. You look amazing."

"Really?" It was entirely possible that Ang was just saying that so Fiona would stop obsessing. If so, it might be working. "Are you sure?"

The eggplant-colored dress had long been one of her favorites. It was short enough to pass for a cocktail dress, with clean, unfussy lines. Ang nodded as Delia knocked on the open door and came into the room, her expression just as captivated as Ang's.

Ang glanced at Delia. "Come on in and have a look at my handiwork."

Ha. Fiona had been the one to climb in and out of four different dresses. But to be fair, Ang had done her hair, and it lay in soft waves across her shoulders. Pivoting with a touch of runway model in her pose, Fiona faced Delia with a smile.

"Perfect," Delia declared and then her mouth drew into a flat line. "But…"

"But?" Fiona repeated. She didn't have time or the energy for buts.

"I have one slight addition for you."

When Delia's face softened, Fiona knew she hadn't really meant there was something lacking. Fiona's lungs hitched as Delia held up a sixteen inch pearl necklace with a pearl drop lavaliere in the center.

As Fiona gasped and fingered the beautiful lavaliere, Delia said, "It was my mother's. I know I'm not your mom and I could never take her place. But…"

Delia clasped the necklace around Fiona's neck. The pearls lay against her skin, cool and smooth. "This is really special."

It was a miracle that her throat had worked. Delia hugged her, causing Ang to squawk.

"Watch the hair!"

Delia and Fiona both laughed and broke apart. Clasping her hand, Delia held it firmly, communicating far more than she had with her small speech. They were tight no matter what went on between father and daughter. It meant everything to Fiona to have Delia as a friend.

"Are you ready?" Delia brushed a tear from her eye. "Let's go. Your fake boyfriend will be here any minute."

Ang took off in pursuit of Brandon, who had asked her to meet him at the back door near the kitchen. Fiona went out the front door to wait on the steps, as instructed by her date for the evening.

Not *date*, her…companion. Friend? She pursed her lips. Derek was her father's chef. That distinction would always be true and might be the best option for his role in her life at this point.

The clop of horse hooves rang out in the night air, unmistakable to someone who had lived a good portion of her life near Central Park.

A white carriage pulled by a fluffy black horse rolled up the circular drive. Enchanted, Fiona watched it draw near and then turn at the bend in the road to reveal an incredibly good looking passenger, whose face broke into a smile as he spied her waiting.

Almost before the carriage completely stopped, Derek vaulted from the seat, spreading his hands wide to encompass the entire vehicle. "Your hansom cab awaits."

"I never expected all of this," Fiona told him in the world's worst *duh* moment. She hadn't expected anything, let alone something so romantic it stole her breath.

Gallantly, he held out his arm and she clasped it, thoroughly caught up in the mood.

Derek jerked his head at the front of the carriage. "The bells were the horse's idea."

"You have gone above and beyond," she said with a laugh that conveyed exactly how pleased she was.

"You said it. A deal's a deal." He helped her into the carriage and as soon as she got settled, he climbed in next to her. "It's not exactly Central Park, but it's not bad."

It was better than not bad. It was amazing. Derek had literally no reason to be so accommodating, not when there was so little chance of her coming through with her half of the deal. The only reason he could possibly have gone to all this trouble was because he wanted to.

What did that mean? Had he started to get confused about what was real and what was fake in their relationship like she had?

Fiona studied him from the corner of her eye as he

spread the heavy wool blanket across her lap and then his. They weren't even touching but the carriage felt cozy and warm.

"It's beautiful," she announced and no, she didn't just mean the scenery. The carriage, the man, the evening. All of it.

"It's the moonlight." Derek glanced heavenward as if that explained the magic here on earth. Even the moonlight was different than in New York. Largely because she could share it with Derek.

"In Vermont," Fiona murmured, thinking of the song.

The horse whinnied and set off at a slow trot. Fiona had no clue what else to expect from Derek this evening, but she did know she couldn't wait to find out.

The MapleDance hit an eleven on a cheese-factor scale of one to ten, from the big cartoon crescent moon hanging from the ceiling to the repurposed white Christmas lights tacked up in long strings. Derek loved every bit of it. Though that might have something to do with his companion more than anything.

Fiona Rangely was, bar none, the most beautiful woman he'd ever met. In that dress, with her face lit up as she surveyed the event hall, she slayed him. Fiona was better than a perfect pie crust, far superior to getting the right crispiness to the bacon in his maple bacon pork loin, and definitely more pleasing to the eye than a clean kitchen at the end of the day.

When he'd booked the carriage, he'd known there was a possibility she might read into it. Hoped she would, honestly. He'd grown a little tired of dancing around his feelings for her. Tonight seemed like a good time to spell some things out. See where the chips fell, so to speak.

"It's so beautiful," Fiona said as they strolled through the center of the room. Jazz music swelled from hidden speakers, set at just the right volume to allow for either dancing or talking, pending the couple's objective for the evening.

Derek intended to do a lot of both. "Amazing what a few twinkly lights can do. You know," he commented as they paused near a giant silver punchbowl set up on a long table. "If I were Nate and I walked in here to find you dressed like this, dancing with some other guy. Well, that just might send me over the edge."

And that was the stone cold truth. Nate was an idiot to have given up Fiona, and it served him right to be over there eating his heart out. Tonight, Derek had a shot and he was taking it.

Fiona smiled. "Are you asking me to dance?"

"If the duck boot fits." He extended his arm, which Fiona took eagerly.

"I'm just staying in character," she explained in a rush as he raised his eyebrows.

Sure. So was he. Except he was playing the part of a character who'd asked Fiona to dance because he wanted to. This wasn't a night of *fake*. Not right now. As he folded Fiona into his arms, he glanced down into her melted chocolate gaze. Normally, he wasn't a betting man, but he'd lay odds she hadn't even noticed Nate and Hailey dancing nearby. Good. He wasn't pointing out the competition, that was for sure.

The band segued into "Moonlight in Vermont."

"I hope a slow song won't be a problem," he said and pulled her a little closer.

She didn't protest, blinking up at him with a misty smile. "I think I'll manage."

They swayed to the dulcet tones of the song playing, gazes locked, and this dance became the most amazing thing they'd done together thus far. There was something different about Fiona tonight, something he couldn't put his finger on, but it didn't seem like she was pretending, either.

Behind her, Hailey had dragged Nate off the dance floor and shoved him into a corner. Her body language had "couple fight" all over it. Nate put his hand on her arm but she jerked away. Uh, oh. Trouble in paradise? Didn't matter. Not his problem.

"You want my opinion?" he said to Fiona and her palm moved up a little higher on his shoulder, drawing them a touch closer.

She laughed. "Do I have a choice?"

"Maybe Nate was just one more thing for you to check off your to-do list."

No going back. He'd laid it out there with succinctness. *Nate's not the guy for you.* It was obvious to practically everyone. Tonight, he'd like to get Fiona on board with that realization too.

"And you want my opinion? You are a surprisingly good dancer."

That was an interesting tell. Instead of agreeing with him, she'd turned the conversation back to him. Which he didn't mind a bit. Nate could fend for himself.

Extending his arm, he twirled her once. "Hey, working in a kitchen is a dance of its own. You're not so bad yourself."

She folded easily back into his embrace. "Thanks."

The music swelled, romantic and beautiful. A fitting tribute to the woman in his arms.

"This is such a beautiful song," she commented, apparently as struck by it as Derek was.

"I love this song," he admitted and sang along with a bit of the verse, locking his gaze on hers as the romantic lyrics spoke for him. "I've got to hand it to you. You're pulling off your Vermont act surprisingly well."

"Can I tell you a secret?" Fiona murmured, lifting her gaze to his, sweeping him up in the moment. "Maybe it's not an act."

That sounded like the greenest green light to him. She'd realized tonight was about being real, about laying it all out there, just as he had. It emboldened him to say exactly what was in his heart.

"You know," he murmured. "When I said earlier I had everything I needed up here. It wasn't entirely true."

"What was missing?"

Gazes locked, a wealth of understanding passed between them. *She* was missing. And somehow, he'd found her. As if pulled by magnets, she lifted her lips, as caught up in the music and the magic of the night as he was. The almost-kiss stirred and grew, and he leaned down to complete the connection. But someone grabbed him by the shoulder, effectively pulling them apart.

Derek blinked at the mayor, still trying to process that he'd interrupted his moment with Fiona.

"Derek," Mayor Slone gushed and pulled him in the opposite direction of the one he wanted to go— toward Fiona. "There are some people here from the governor's staff that I'd love for you to meet."

People? People who weren't Fiona had no shot of holding his interest. Nor did he want to do anything with the mayor.

"I'm sorry," he mouthed to her.

"It's okay," she murmured back, her expression a little crushed, which went a long way toward salving his own disappointment.

The second he could untangle himself from this meet and greet, he'd find her and pick up that kiss where it had left off. Nothing else could be allowed to get in the way of finally connecting with Fiona for real.

173

At loose ends with Derek off schmoozing the people from the governor's office, Fiona wandered over to the punchbowl. Just as she picked up a glass of what appeared to be cider, Nate materialized at her elbow.

Great. What did it say about her state of mind that he was literally the last person she wanted to see? Sure he looked handsome in his dark suit. He'd always been magazine-cover worthy with his swept back dark hair and natural style. But he really couldn't hold a candle to Derek's open and easy-on-the-eyes good looks.

"Fancy meeting you here," Nate said with a charming smile. "I've been wanting to talk to you all night."

She noticed he didn't have a familiar pink-clad woman on his arm. "Okay."

"Look, I know Derek's a nice guy and all. But it's not serious between you two, is it?"

"I don't know." And that was the truth, not some cagey answer designed to make Nate jealous or whatever stupid agenda she'd had in mind when coming up with the fake relationship deal. "Why?"

"Don't you see it, Fiona?" Nate took her hand in his and she was so shocked, she let him. "We both rebounded and bounced right back into each other. It's Destiny."

No, *she* had not rebounded. She had worked on a desperate plan to win him back, but now that it seemed to be succeeding, her heart wasn't quite in it like she'd thought it would be. "Nate, I'm confused. What about Hailey?"

"She stormed off. She's headed back to New York. It's over. I was going to tell her how I feel about you, but apparently she figured it out."

Oh. That poor woman. She'd been treated terribly, when she'd only wanted to show her boyfriend around Vermont. The sick little wave in Fiona's stomach convicted her. That had been the fallout of Fiona's plan—Hailey had gotten hurt.

Granted, Nate was the fickle one who had entered into a relationship with Hailey of his own free will, then realized he'd made a mistake. That wouldn't have happened if Nate had truly been over Fiona in the first place, *before* he'd started dating someone new.

But still. It didn't make her feel any better to have been a party to breaking up a couple while on vacation. Hailey was probably a nice person who hadn't deserved to be caught up in dumb games.

Nate smiled and gripped both of her hands in his, a tender expression on his face. Exactly as she'd pictured back when her goal had been to win him back. For some reason, she felt nothing.

"Let's go back to the city," he suggested. "And pick up where we left off. It was always us, Fiona. At any speed."

Wow.

He'd fallen for Vermont Fiona's act too. Like her father had, they both assumed that she'd slowed down because she'd learned a few lessons and they liked that idea. Only Derek knew the real score. She had to be *enticed* to slow down. Given something to make it

175

worth her while. Badgered into it, honestly, with style and grace, by someone who paid enough attention to her to figure out exactly how to do that.

Someone like Derek.

Nate *had* been a checkbox. Or more to the point, an accessory to a New York real estate broker. He went with her perception of herself, a busy, focused career woman. He did not go with the real Fiona. He couldn't. She didn't even know the real Fiona, but she had a feeling Derek had his finger on that pulse more so than anyone else. "I'm sorry. I have to go."

Stumbling through the crowd, she spied Derek still speaking to some VIP types with that government-employee look about them, as if they had important things going on all hours of the day. She waited until he looked up and then waved to him. Nodding, he extracted himself from the crowd, but he hadn't smiled at her once.

Something felt…off. They'd just danced together not too long ago, and she'd like to do it again. But that didn't seem to be in the cards as she took in Derek's remote expression. Was he upset about something one of the governor's people had said to him?

Regardless, the magic of the evening seemed to have vanished.

"I'm ready to go," she told him instead of asking him to dance again, like she'd planned. Her emotions had risen up in her throat like a tight ball and she didn't want to examine them.

Derek bundled her into the carriage and as the

horse rolled it away from the MapleDance, she decided to address the elephant in the room. "You're sure quiet tonight."

"Just thinking." Derek pursed his lips. "So. Looks like you got Nate back."

"What do you mean?" Had Nate gone behind her back and said something to Derek? Was that why he was upset?

"I saw you two together holding hands."

Her heart froze as Derek's remote expression took on new meaning. He'd seen that little episode with Nate. And clearly, it hadn't pleased him to see her with another man, particularly not the one she'd made such a fuss over. "Oh that? He just grabbed my hand."

"And I'd say that was a 'tell.'" He stared out over the dark, hushed landscape. "Does this mean you're headed back to the city?"

"No, I can't."

"Why not?"

Because I thought I'd stick around and see if you and I might have something to talk about. But she couldn't say that, not with the weird vibe between them. "I still haven't held up my end of the bargain."

"Don't worry. I think we can consider our deal complete."

"No. I haven't gotten you your field yet! And I never break a promise."

"It's okay. I'm letting you off the hook."

Why wasn't he fighting for her? He'd always thrown his weight around, acting like he knew what was best for her. But in this, he backed off? "What if I don't want you to? And what about what you said to me tonight at the dance?"

The "something missing" from his Vermont life was *her*. There was no possible way to misinterpret that. Was there?

"Maybe we both got swept up in the moment." Derek finally glanced at her and some of the tenderness of earlier returned. For all the good it served. He was essentially telling her he'd messed up and said some things he regretted. That he hadn't been serious.

Apparently she'd had revelations about both Nate *and* Derek with incomplete information. Derek wasn't the man for her, either. She'd fallen for the pretense, just as he had, but he'd realized it sooner.

"My feet are planted here," he told her gently. "And yours are in New York. That's just who we are, right?"

There was so much more to it than that and she tried to think of how to explain it as he helped her down from the carriage. "Of course, but—"

"You deserve everything you've worked so hard for."

Which was in New York. She stared at him, trying desperately to figure out if that meant he was shutting down the entire conversation because he liked her but hated New York so he was out.

"Yes, young man." A deeper male voice from behind her cut into Derek's speech. "I completely agree."

She whirled. And blinked. "*Irwin*. What are you doing here?"

It was Irwin. Standing on the steps of her father's inn. In Vermont. Everything swirled together in her head and then unspooled at an alarming pace. Bad, bad timing.

Her dad's old friend smiled. "I'll be the first to admit, I don't usually have to work this hard to recruit top talent. But I'm also not someone who gives up easily. Perhaps you and I can discuss the terms of our contract over a late dinner?"

Derek's face closed in. "I'll get something started for you."

So that was that, apparently. He *was* out. She watched him trudge up the stairs, feeling very much like something had just slipped through her fingers before she'd realized she wanted to hang onto it.

"Shall we?" Irwin held out his arm, oblivious to the crushing sensation in her chest.

He'd chased her down because like Derek and even Nate, Irwin assumed her heart was in New York, and she needed a reminder that Vermont Fiona didn't exist. It was all an act. One she'd fallen for harder than anyone else.

Hadn't she learned anything from her father? Emotions led to trouble. She'd let hers off the leash and now look. All the signs pointed to heartache if she kept going down this path. New York Fiona made sense. To everyone.

Squaring her shoulders, she took Irwin's arm and went inside to get her heart aligned with her head.

FOURTEEN

The next morning, Fiona went for her typical early morning jog in the snow, but the hushed landscape invited her to slow down and savor the scenery, the feel of Vermont. Maybe she'd been missing things in New York by being in such a rush all the time. If nothing else, she could embrace the lessons she'd learned here when she went back home.

Her feet turned toward Chauncey's farm automatically, and true to form, the old man stood out by his barn, his face implacable as she approached.

"Returning to the scene of the crime?" He nodded at the fence that stretched between them.

"At least you didn't tear it down," she returned.

"Well, I thought about it. But the durn thing is too well built."

Fiona hid a smile. That was as close to a thanks as she was likely to get. But she'd take it from such a tough customer. "Honestly, sir, we were just trying to do something nice. I'm sorry if we overreached. I'm headed out of town soon. But I got to hand it to you.

You're on a very short list of sellers who I couldn't budge."

Chauncey almost grinned. "That so?"

"Look. How about we call it even? There's a big dinner at the Inn tonight." She dug around in her jacket pocket until she found one of Brandon's flyers and pulled it out to hand to him. "I'd love for you to check it out. Tell my Dad that I asked you to stop by. It's my treat. Don't you owe it to yourself to at least give it a try?"

He didn't crumple it up and stomp on it, which frankly had been expected. After reading the whole thing twice, he glanced up at her but said nothing else. She nodded and waved at the cow. "Bye, Bessie."

Likely Chauncey would trash the flyer after she walked off, but she resisted the urge to turn around and confirm. This wasn't her fight any longer and she had to concede with grace.

When she got back to the inn, she saw Delia setting out silverware in the dining room. She wandered in, already sad that she had to leave her stepmother behind in a few short hours.

"Hey," Delia called when she caught sight of Fiona. "How was your run?"

"It kind of turned into more of a walk." By design. "I just wanted to have one last look around before I head back to the city later today."

Because Delia was Delia, she zeroed in on Fiona's face, her own smile slipping a bit with her overall evaluation. "Is something wrong, dear?"

All at once, Fiona's eyelids pricked with unshed tears. At least someone had noticed that she didn't have it all together. "Irwin brought up a draft of the contract and it's... I mean, this job is a once-in-a-lifetime opportunity."

"Well, where's the smile then?"

Trust Delia to realize there was a reason she wasn't quite able to get her lips to curve up. "I just—between Nate and the job and—" Derek. Vermont. *Everything*. "I don't know what I want anymore."

Worst of all, there wasn't even a decision to be made here. Nate wasn't right for her anymore, if he ever was, and Derek wasn't offering her anything.

So why did everything feel so unsettled? Why wasn't it easy for her to go back to her real life?

"Irwin wants me to sign right when I get back to the city." And she should. He'd been more than patient.

"Well, don't rush a decision," Delia advised. "In your heart, you'll know what's best."

"Oh, no. I've already decided. I told Irwin I accepted the job. He's just tweaking some terms of the contract and it'll be time to sign." Assuming she could get her hand to hold a pen without shaking. What was *wrong* with her? The walk this morning had unraveled her or something. "I better go pack."

Before she could escape to her room to nurse her mood, Harris stormed into the lobby, hands waving. "We have a problem."

Harris and Delia joined Derek's nightmare just as he hung up the phone. Not only had his bubble completely burst when it came to Fiona, the most important dinner of his career had just blown up in his face.

Nightmare might be too tame of a word for the disaster unfolding at an alarming clip.

"What is it?" Delia asked, clearly picking up on the black vibe in the kitchen.

"A truck jackknifed. The road is closed between here and Montpelier." Delia's gasp nearly cut him off, but he continued through the tight knot in his throat. Somehow. His employers needed to hear the entire grim truth. "There's nothing getting through for hours, including half my ingredients and all the extra kitchen staff I hired."

Harris gripped the edge of the granite island that dominated the kitchen, his knuckles white. "What are we looking at?"

Derek grimaced and opted to be heartbreakingly honest, though whose heart would be the most broken, he couldn't say. "I've got no sous chef. I've got no extra staff. Half my ingredients are stuck in traffic. I'm sorry, Harris. I think we gotta cancel."

"Cancel?" Harris laughed but no one mistook it for amusement. "We can't cancel. We have half the food bloggers in New England upstairs, and they're going to want dinner. And with Irwin here, my humiliation will be complete."

Yeah, there was a lot of that going around. Irwin

had put the final nail in Derek's coffin by showing up in the nick of time to remind Fiona of what she had waiting for her back in New York. She couldn't get to that late dinner fast enough last night so she and her new boss could hammer out the terms of her contract with him.

He hadn't meant to overhear anything, least of all how truly spectacular of an offer Irwin had made Fiona. But if she hadn't wanted Derek to know every last detail of her success, she wouldn't have met with Irwin in the dining room where voices carried straight into the kitchen.

How could he blame her for embracing a great job in a city she loved? She was probably halfway back to New York by now—

But, no. She walked into the kitchen. "No one is cancelling anything."

Fiona's voice washed over him and he turned to see her standing just behind Harris in a purple jogging suit that reminded him of her dress from the night before. Why, he had no clue other than he'd been thinking about her in that dress non-stop since then.

"I thought you were headed back to the city," he said.

That had come out all wrong. What he'd meant to say was, *what do you care?* And because he hadn't said that, he was very much afraid he'd tipped his hand. Now she might guess that he'd been convinced she'd left without saying goodbye and hadn't been handling it well.

She should have gone. With Nate. They belonged together. Seeing Fiona with him at the dance had solidified it in his mind. Derek had let himself get caught up in the romance of the week, none of which had been real, and that was that. He couldn't afford to get lost in something fake again. It was too hard when it all came crashing down.

"I am," she said and no—*that* was the final nail in his coffin. "But first, I think we have a dinner to pull off."

"We?" Harris asked.

"Yes," Fiona responded like it was obvious what she'd meant. "Me, you, Delia, Angela. We'll all help out."

Her earnestness clutched at his heart. Or maybe that was his optimism flaring up in spite of it all— as if she might really care about his professional crisis. "That's sweet. But none of you have any real experience."

"You're good with details. I'm good with speed," she reminded him. As if he'd forget. "You're going to need both."

"What about all of my ingredients?"

"Forget the menu." She waved that off, oblivious to the fact that the menu was like his roadmap. "We'll work with what we have."

"Yeah," Delia said as she hopped onboard the crazy train. "The general store is going to have things."

"Exactly." Fiona stabbed the air in Delia's direction. "They'll have things and we'll just improvise the rest.

What about your family's famous recipes? You could use those."

Her enthusiasm caught him by the throat, and the barest glimmer of hope filtered through the bleakness of the situation. He *could* possibly use his grandma's recipes. Maybe. The knot in his stomach loosened just a touch as he let his mind wander through the dishes that he knew like the back of his hand.

Sure, none of it was fancy Michelin-starred chef type fare. But he had generations of Vermont blood in his veins and those recipes did too. That had to count for something.

He might be down but he was not out.

"Okay." And with that, he started to believe in himself again. Because she'd believed in him first. It wasn't fair for her to be so wonderful and so out of reach. "Fiona, you don't have to do this."

"It's the least I can do." Her big brown eyes sought and held his. "And then we'll call our deal even."

Oh, right. Of course this was about the deal. Not because she cared, but because she had a righteous sense of fair play. *Shake it off.* He had some improvising to do. "Okay."

Harris and Delia glanced at each other, their relief obvious. They believed in him too, and that went a long way. Fiona rounded up Angela and Brandon and once all his recruits were assembled, he started giving out orders to the apron-clad troops.

"Delia." He pointed to the lady at the head of the line. "We'll have you working the front of the house."

No brainer since that was what she normally did.

"Brandon, Angela, after you're done with salads and prep, we'll move you over to serving. If you think you can work together."

"We do," they said at the same time with smiles that said not only could they, but it would be a pleasure.

"Fiona and Harris, we'll have you on the line," he concluded. With that organized, he could turn his thoughts to the important part of the evening—the food. "Okay, now for the menu. Tortiere would be good."

"What's tortiere?" Fiona asked.

"Meat pie," he translated even as he visualized how he could make it worthy of more sophisticated palates. The food bloggers visited top tier restaurants on a regular basis and he couldn't afford to skimp on one single detail. "French settlers brought it over from Quebec. It's very delicious, very Vermont. My grandma had an amazing one."

"Oh, what about Anadama bread?" Fiona suggested and instantly he liked that idea.

"Yes. And fiddlehead ferns," he threw in as his creative inspiration rolled out the entire menu in seconds flat. "I think this just might work. Pure Vermont home cooking raised to fine dining."

He and Fiona were good together. *In the kitchen*, he stressed to himself.

"Yes." Fiona nodded. "It's like the Yankee credo. Make do with what you have."

"Let's bring it in."

Derek stuck his hand in the center of the group and they all piled on top, cheering as their hands connected in a show of solidarity. Everyone moved to their assigned roles, but they had so little experience, he had to guide practically every move. Not his normal way to operate, but necessary, and he didn't really mind. Except everywhere he turned, he ran into Fiona and she never missed an opportunity to smile at him, which made everything better. And worse.

"Work together, everyone," he called out to the helpers. "We have to sync up like an assembly line. If we get behind on even one item, we'll back up the next fifty dishes."

Harris glanced at his daughter as they chopped side by side. "Us cooking together, it kind of takes me back."

"Remember Sunday barbecues on the balcony, your steaks, Mom's potatoes, my brownies?"

"How could I forget?"

Derek hated to interrupt as it felt like they were having a good moment together. But this was do or die time. "Okay, we've got two hours till the guests start arriving in the dining room. Let's get prepping."

Delia came in from her trip to the local market, carrying a basket full of fresh vegetables. Nothing fancy, some carrots and squash, but vital items. He smiled his gratitude and concentrated on the meat he had browning at the stove. This was a delicate dance, like he'd told Fiona last night, and he had to get it right. For the inn. But also for his own professional integrity.

The food bloggers weren't just going to skewer the Inn at Swan Lake if he failed. It would be his reputation smeared as well. So he wouldn't fail.

In the course of all the prep work and rushing around, he bumped into Fiona four times. All four times, her smile caught him in the gut. Why couldn't things be different? They worked so seamlessly together. But instead of pointing that out, he'd chosen to let her go. After all, he'd lost her to the city for good.

No. In all actuality, he'd never really had her—their relationship had been one hundred percent fake. He'd fallen for someone who didn't exist. Vermont wasn't but a short blip to Fiona. That almost-kiss last night? Ill-advised. Good thing he'd been interrupted before he'd gotten a taste of what he had to give up.

Judging by those heavy, meaningful glances Angela and Brandon kept exchanging, someone's love life had taken a turn for the better in Vermont. Just not his.

Two hours passed in a blur, and guests started filtering in. Delia handled it with her usual style, not that Derek had more than a half second to peek out to gauge the crowd. Both dining rooms were full to the brim—a good sign. Lots of expectant faces. Also a good sign.

Back in the kitchen, he supervised Fiona and Harris as they plated, then handed courses to Angela and Brandon. They worked like a finely-tuned machine, a blessing, considering. His hired staff may not have even worked so well together.

Brandon came into the kitchen with a slightly dazed expression. "You are never going to guess who just showed up. Chauncey."

"*What*?" Derek glanced at Fiona and then back at Brandon. "Why?"

This he had to see for himself. He wiped his hands and strode to the pass-through between the kitchen and the dining room, where he could view the tables but no one could see him. Sure enough, the old man had just settled into a seat, looking ill at ease and out of place in a maroon sweater instead of his usual plaid.

What madness was this? Had Chauncey come to sabotage the blogger's dinner by bad-mouthing the inn, Derek and everyone named Rangely? How had the old man even heard about tonight's important event?

"Oh," Fiona said with a nervous laugh as she peeked over his shoulder. "I went over to apologize and invited him to be our guest."

Which she'd done with literally no heads-up to the chef who had everything on the line. He couldn't be mad, though. Fiona had meant well.

Derek backed into the kitchen, feeling as dazed as Brandon had looked. "I can't believe he said yes."

"He's a thrifty New Englander," Fiona said. "A free meal is a free meal."

Yeah, but still. He couldn't help but think Chauncey wouldn't hesitate to feed Derek to the wolves if given the chance. He dismissed that from his mind because he had to in order to get the rest of the evening in the bag. The food had to be perfect; he turned himself inside out to make that happen. As did everyone else, and he couldn't help but be grateful for their dedication.

Finally, the rush died down and Derek was able to steal a few moments with Fiona. He poured her a glass of wine and then himself. "How do you think it's going?"

"I don't know," she said. "Maybe we survived?"

"Well, I couldn't have done it without you." And he meant that in more ways than one. She'd inspired him, cheered him on, kept his motivation high. It was everything. He clinked his glass to hers as he sank into the seat next to her. "To speed."

She smiled. "And yet taking the time to do things right."

Delia broke apart the moment as she rushed into the kitchen. "Excuse me, but Chauncey is insisting on having a word with you."

That did not sound fun. What was he in for now, another ear-blistering tirade about the elements he'd been attracting? Why not? Chauncey had gotten a firsthand look at the inn and its guests. He'd likely gleaned all sorts of new fodder to feed his hatred of the changing landscape of the valley.

Derek and Fiona glanced at each other and she shook her head slightly. "Be my guest."

"You invited him," he reminded her with a touch more desperation than he would have liked.

"Oh, come on," she murmured. "Okay. Fine. We're in this together."

"Where's my hockey helmet when I need it?" Derek climbed to his feet and Fiona followed him into the dining room.

Chauncey stood holding his coat, staring around the dining room as if he'd accidentally wandered into enemy territory and couldn't quite figure out why he hadn't been blown to bits by a hidden land mine.

Not a promising sign.

"We're in for it," he whispered to Fiona.

"Mr. Chauncey," Fiona said with a genuine smile because that was what she did—smiled in the face of adversity. "Was everything okay?"

"Okay?" He shifted from foot to foot and finally blurted, "It was delicious. Best meal I've had in years."

"Really?" Derek couldn't stop his mouth from turning up.

"Anyone who can cook a dinner like that is okay in my book. Keeping Vermont traditions alive." Chauncey nodded once.

"I... Than—thank you," Derek stuttered.

What irony. The only reason he'd pulled together that particular menu was due to the jackknifed eighteen wheeler. Otherwise, the dinner would have been completely different. And likely not as big of a hit with the crusty old farmer.

It felt like a victory regardless of what happened

with the professional reviewers who had also been in attendance tonight.

Having said his piece, Chauncey pushed between them, clearly ready to leave. But then he turned at the door. "Someone said to me recently that good fences make good neighbors. That might be true. That field. It's yours if you still want it."

"Yes," he choked out. Somehow. He held out his hand to Chauncey, who clasped it firmly. It was a deal. A solid, real deal on the field.

"Bring by the papers tomorrow," Chauncey instructed and strode for the door.

With a surprised chuckle, Fiona glanced at Derek. "Did that just happen?"

"I think so." Before he could check the impulse, he'd swept Fiona up in an embrace. A celebratory hug. She felt nice in his arms.

Someone cleared their throat. They broke apart and he turned to see Irwin and Nate still sitting in the dining room, apparently witness to the whole encounter. Derek would not have hugged Fiona if he'd known other people had been in the room, especially not Nate.

Derek knew firsthand what it felt like to see a woman you thought you had something special with in the company of the man you were painfully aware was your competition for her affections.

"Excuse me," Irwin said. "My compliments to the chef."

"To both of them," Nate corrected with a smug smile at Derek and then Fiona.

"I have to say that dinner was worth the extra day." Irwin lifted his wine glass to Derek and then grinned as Harris came into the room. "Now, I intend to beat my old rival in a game of bridge. Harris?"

"You're on." Fiona's father took off his apron and folded it over his arm. "I'll bid seven, no trump, and you'll go back to the city with an empty wallet."

"Yeah. Good luck with that." Irwin skirted the table to join Harris, but before they left the room, he paused and turned to Fiona. "I'm leaving first thing in the morning. You, young lady, have a contract to sign in my office tomorrow."

"I'll be there," she promised and Irwin pumped his fist in victory. He and Harris strolled from the room, obviously in hog heaven over their impending bridge game.

Everything was falling into place for Fiona. The dinner had gone off without a hitch and there was no reason for her to delay returning to the city. She glanced back at Derek with a searching expression on her face that nearly tore his heart from his chest. They both needed some type of closure here. "I guess we both got what we wanted."

"Yeah." Her smile trembled a bit but he didn't ask why. Not his business.

"Thanks again for your help today."

"My pleasure."

And that was that. Nate stood, stepping away

from the table in a well cut suit, and obviously he'd been waiting for Fiona to finish up so they could…do whatever. Live happily ever after.

"I'll leave you to it," he told her and turned away.

What else was there to say other than goodbye?

FIFTEEN

Fiona watched Derek walk away, quite unable to forget he'd just hugged her. Her arms still tingled where he'd touched her and she wished for a second she could call him back to start that hug all over.

But he'd made his position clear. There was no room for compromise in Derek Price's world. So be it.

"So," Nate said pleasantly. "I was thinking if we start back early enough, we can beat the traffic."

She stared at him, her brain having real difficulty processing what he'd just said. Had he been *waiting* for her? Well, duh, obviously. Ugh, this was all her fault for leaving him at the dance and not making herself clear then.

Maybe she hadn't fully cut him off then because she'd truly still been waffling about New York Fiona and how that all fit together. Nate had been a huge part of that. But he couldn't be any longer.

"Nate, I need to tell you... We both need to move on."

"Move on?" His face crinkled as he internalized what she meant.

"I'm headed back to the city with a fresh start. And this new job is going to be twice the juggling."

"Yeah, we'll make it work." The sincerity in his tone had her shaking her head.

Like you made it work last time? He didn't even see the irony in his statement. Nate wasn't a forever kind of guy, and she'd seen exactly how fast he ditched Hailey, who'd given him *all* of her attention. If Fiona did agree to a second chance, how much faster would he get tired of her not making time for him? *Fast.* He didn't even know what he wanted.

"No, Nate," she said firmly. He needed to get this straight, once and for all. "I'm sure of this. I came up here to clear my head and I did. You were right. You deserve the right girl. I'm afraid that girl isn't me."

Not now, if she ever had been. She left him standing in the inn's dining room and went to her room feeling as if a weight had been lifted. After a great night's sleep, she woke early and started packing. Nate had been right about one thing—the early bird missed the traffic and she had an appointment with Irwin to sign the contract for her new job.

Somehow, it wasn't as exciting of a thought as it had been the day before.

Angela woke to the sound of something plinking against her window. She rolled from the bed to glance outside and lo and behold—Brandon stood out in the snow, tossing pebbles at the glass. He grinned and waved her down.

A clandestine meeting at dawn with Brandon? *Yes, please.* She and Fiona had talked about leaving today and Angela had been dreading it. This thing with Brandon had barely gotten started thanks to his middle name being Molasses. Whatever was happening between them was still in the delicate, fragile stage where blowing on it too hard might break it apart. She'd been pretending everything would fall into place. If she couldn't believe in the magic of Vermont, what could she believe in?

But then Brandon had left her after dinner last night with a murmured, "Good night." Then nothing. No next steps. No declarations of any sort. She'd gone to bed thinking that she'd struck out again.

Breathless, she dove into some clothes, wrapped her coat around her and jammed a knit hat down over her wild red curls. Who had time for curl taming when a cute boy wanted you to sneak out with him?

Except it was six a.m. and Angela had been an adult for quite some time, one who came and went as she pleased. This was nothing but pure adventure and might be one of the most exciting things that had ever happened to her.

Anything could happen. Or nothing. But the possibilities…

Brandon waited for her at the bottom of the steps off the main porch, clad in a heavy coat and scarf, cheeks already red, which told her he'd been outside for more than a couple of minutes. Getting up his courage to wake her? Nah. Chopping wood for the inn's fireplace, most likely.

"Hey," he said, his eyes crinkling. "Want to walk with me down to the pond?"

"Of course." It was cold, still a little dark and the pond was likely frozen. What wasn't to like about that plan? She got to spend precious time with Brandon, time that had been draining away at a rapid clip, and she had nothing at her disposal to stop the clock.

Nor did she have any reason to think that he wanted her to. Maybe he just wanted to say a long goodbye and shove her out the door toward New York. Who could figure him out?

As they meandered down the hill, Brandon made an effort to match her stride, which she appreciated. He moved as if he'd been born to this rugged landscape, with confidence and sure steps. She had to pick her way carefully lest she slip on a patch of icy snow.

"Thanks for not thinking the pebbles on your window was weird," he told her just as the pond came into view through the skinny bare trees.

"No! It was inventive." She laughed. "Most people would knock on the door or send a text message. No one has ever gotten my attention with such flair."

He glanced at her sideways. "I don't have your phone number."

That was a telling comment and it fluttered in her stomach that he'd go out of his way to make the point. She might be thirty, but that didn't make her immune to the effects of a nice guy asking for her phone number. "I'll write it down for you when we get back. Cell service is tricky out here."

"I'm aware." He elbowed her lightly. "Hence the pebbles."

"Thanks for not letting me leave without seeing you again," she shot back, feeling fairly safe that due to her impending departure, she could be honest with him about what she was feeling at this point. "I'm a little sad to be leaving already. Feels like we just got here."

"That's an easy fix." Brandon paused at the edge of the lake and stared out over it. "Don't leave."

Agape, she blinked at his stoic profile. "Like ever?"

What had just happened? Was he asking her to *stay*? Like *stay* stay, as in because of him?

He shrugged and laughed. "Sure, you can leave some day. But just not now. I'd like to show you around town some. Take you on a real date."

Well, calling a spade a spade seemed to be the order of the day. A glow exploded in her chest as she vigorously shook her head up and down. "I would like that. *Oh*. But no, I can't."

Gak, what rotten timing. Fiona needed to be back in the city to sign the contract with Irwin. *Disaster*. She was Angela's ride.

Brandon's face went blank. "Okay. Well, it was a

last minute invitation. I'm sure you have other, more important—"

"I want to," she broke in. "But the rental car is Fiona's. I have no way of getting back to the city without her."

His shoulders relaxed and turned to her, sweeping her hand up in his. "Also an easy fix. Say: Brandon, will you drive me back to New York later?"

She laughed and parroted his statement, her pulse pounding. The gloves she wore didn't really let her enjoy the fact that Brandon still held her hand. But that didn't seem to matter to the squishy place inside her.

"Then that's a done deal." He let his gaze linger over her face. "As long as you want to stay."

"I do. We have a lot of catching up to do."

And out of nowhere, he pulled on her hand until their lips met and he kissed her. Brandon was *kissing* her! The cold semi-darkness ceased to matter as they sealed the deal there by the frozen pond. Brandon Rangely had finally made his move and Angela was right there to meet him halfway.

Angela came back from wherever she'd been hiding. Great timing.

"Hey," Fiona called. "Are you packed yet? I'm supposed to meet Irwin in his office first thing to sign the contract. You know what? I'm glad we came up here. It was the right call."

"Shake things up a little?" Ang suggested with a wink.

"Yeah. It did." Significantly. Fiona had a new perspective that she'd have never gotten any other way, especially when it came to checking boxes in the boyfriend category, like she'd done with Nate. No more of that.

Next time, it would be for real. Never again would she fabricate a relationship out of thin air—like the one she'd had with Nate. That had been a pure figment of her imagination. They'd occasionally gone out together, sure, but their relationship had zero substance. *He* had zero substance.

Not like the solid, amazing chef she'd met. Now that she had a comparison, there was none.

"Fiona." Ang hesitated, twisting her fingers together as if she couldn't quite figure out what to do with her hands. "Would you mind if I stayed up here a little longer? Brandon wants to show me around."

Which was code for "spend time together." An instant grin nearly cracked Fiona's jaw. "My brother and my best friend? Of course not. I'm happy for you. I mean, it's a little weird, but…"

She threw her arms around Ang to hide the fact that she was blubbering a touch.

Ang stepped back. "Have you had a chance to say goodbye to Derek?"

Fiona took her time wrapping a scarf around

her neck as she worked through how to answer that without sounding needy. "He didn't give me a chance to. No, he'd already taken off early this morning. I'm going to go say goodbye to my dad."

"Good idea."

Ang let her go, thankfully opting to skip the psychoanalysis this time. Fiona didn't need anyone else in her head telling her there was a reason Derek hadn't waited around this morning to see her off—he didn't want to. That relationship wasn't real either and she had no call to wish that it was. The Nate Lesson had stuck deep.

She found her dad in the barn, feeding the horses. Strolling along with him, she watched him pour a scooper full of grain into a trough.

Over his shoulder, he called out, "I can't believe we pulled last night off."

"I know. What a night. It was just a roaring success." For once, he'd opted not to start in on her about why she didn't love the inn, and Fiona was grateful enough for the reprieve to go along with whatever subject he chose.

"Well, we'll have to see what the bloggers say," her father commented. "But regardless, in large part, we've got you to thank."

That choked her up a little. It was nice, this feeling of being a part of something that had real, lasting results. "Oh, Dad. Come on. It was a team effort."

"I think it was more than that."

Fiona cut the conversation short before he geared

up enough to mention how great of a team they were and couldn't she see herself hanging around? "I think I should probably head out."

Harris nodded and pulled her into a hug. "Promise me you'll come and visit more often."

"I'll try, Dad." At his raised eyebrows, she amended that with, "I really will! And you know what, you and Delia should meet me in the city sometime. As much as you don't like it there."

Her father flinched. "Is that what you think?"

"Well…yeah." She glanced around. "Look how far you moved just to get away. From everything. From our apartment. The past. Our lives together."

Especially the places that they'd shared with her mom. That was what really hurt. That he'd so easily given it all up, as if her mom had never existed. How else did you keep memories alive other than to hang on to the places where they'd been created?

"Honey." Harris sighed. "I know how much you loved the apartment. But I got a secret for you. So did I. Noise and all."

Incredulous, Fiona stared at him, waiting for the punchline. He didn't recant. "Then why did you sell it the first chance you got?"

"It was your mom's idea to sell." After he dropped that bombshell, his eyes softened with sincerity and she could tell he believed what he was saying. "She wanted to move up here eventually. She even found this place."

What? That wasn't right. It couldn't be. "Mom loved the city."

"Yeah, she did. You want to know why? Because *we* were there." He circled his hand between them. "Look, when your mom passed away, I knew it was time to live that dream. For both of us, since she was gone. I only wish we'd done it sooner."

This was...something else. The walls around Fiona's heart cracked and fell away as she absorbed his words. She'd had it all wrong—*wrong*—this whole time. Furthermore, he'd kept this secret for *years,* letting her think he'd done something so unforgivable.

She processed it some more and then choked out, "Why have you never told me this before?"

"I know how much you loved the old place. And, well..." He shrugged. "I guess I'm just not very good at dealing with emotions."

She had some grace left over to laugh at that. "Yeah. That runs in the family."

Wow. All this time... She'd been living under a false assumption because she'd never really laid it on the line and told her dad what she'd been thinking, why she was so hurt. Explained her feelings.

What else was she missing out on for the same reason? After all, she'd failed to tell Nate in no uncertain terms that they were through at the dance. She'd had to rehash it all over again later. And just maybe, she'd failed to do that with the other man she couldn't seem to get out of her head as well.

Why hadn't she? Fear of her emotions? Derek

deserved better than a fraidy cat who shied away from something wonderful out of some misguided sense that emotions weren't her forte.

"When I was on Wall Street, satisfaction was outfoxing Irwin in some kind of business deal." Chuckling incredulously, her father spread his hands to encompass the expansive grounds around him. "I never imagined that running an inn in Vermont could be so much more satisfying. I guess you can surprise yourself."

She nodded as his meaning sank in. He was saying she could take that lesson as well, look around and really define what satisfaction meant for her. That it was okay to make different decisions based on your heart, not your head. For the first time, she took in the beauty around her, the clean air, the slower pace, the love and family here, and truly considered what it might be like to embrace Vermont Fiona permanently.

Because that was a part of her. A real, live part of her that Derek had uncovered. It wasn't fake, like she'd convinced herself. That had been fear talking. What if she could be brave, like her dad?

It put butterflies in her stomach—maybe the good kind. But also some of the scared-out-of-her-mind kind. "Dad, how did you know you'd end up being happy here?"

He lifted his shoulders. "Sometimes you just have a feeling."

Like the one that she'd had at the dance. And while helping Derek make dinner. That feeling said they had all the right ingredients, but she'd been too focused on what she thought her life should look like rather than what she *wanted* it to look like.

Still checking boxes. "I think I know what you mean."

Some things really were that simple.

The bucket Derek had set up to catch syrup from his tree had nearly filled to the brim. Good thing he'd come by to check on it this morning. Though it had been serendipity that he'd chosen to come here rather than design; he couldn't stick around the inn and watch Fiona walk out of his life. With Nate, no less.

So his tree had won the toss on where he'd go to avoid feeling like the best thing about Vermont had just vanished.

The woods maintained their hush, especially this early in the morning. So the crunch of someone else's footfalls easily echoed through the trees, and he glanced up to see a familiar purple-clad figure. The last person he'd expected to see.

"Fiona." Miracle that his throat had worked. She was so beautiful out here against the backdrop of trees asleep for the winter. "I thought you'd be halfway to Times Square by now."

She wasn't. She was *here*.

"Couldn't leave without checking on our tree."

Except she wasn't looking at the tree. Her gaze stayed firmly fastened on him even as she put her arm around the trunk. "It's funny, I used to think the most important thing was the building. The city. The location. That's part of the reason I got into real estate."

He nodded. "Yeah."

That was the reason he had to let her go. She belonged where it made sense to her to live her life— in the city. There weren't a lot of buildings for sale here, nor people to buy and sell them. She belonged in a different world, one that made her happy.

"I realized something up here."

"What's that?" he prompted when she hesitated.

"It doesn't matter whether it's Manhattan or Vermont. It's not the place that's important. It's the people. It's the memories that make the place really special. Not the building." She met his gaze. "I think I could be happy up here."

That was a complete about face that he could hardly process.

But in her eyes, he saw a wide ocean of things he wanted to understand better. So he got a lot closer, putting a hand on the same tree trunk to balance himself as they connected via the bark. "What about Nate?"

It would have been preferable to never utter his name again, but they had to clear this up, once and for all. Their whole relationship had bloomed under the premise that she wanted to get him back.

"He went back to the city. Alone." A wealth of meaning passed between them as he soaked up her words. She glanced down for the first time, noticing the bucket in his hands. "Hey, that's a pretty good haul."

"Yeah." He chuckled. "I told you good things come with time."

"They certainly do."

The metaphor perfectly described their fake relationship. Given enough time, it had turned into something real and finally he could do the one thing he'd been unable to thus far. He leaned forward and claimed her lips in a sweet kiss.

So this was what it felt like to kiss her the right way. Slowly. With meaning.

Fiona hadn't left. She'd tracked him down solely to tell him she understood that his roots were in Vermont and that was okay because she'd learned to love it here too. Enough to stay.

Time would tell if she'd slowed down for good or if he'd be forced to speed up to stay by her side. But he trusted that she'd wait for him if that was the case and that they'd figure it out together.

When Fiona and Derek strolled back into the inn—as a *couple*—her dad and Delia were at the reservation desk reading something on Delia's e-reader tablet.

"Honey!" Her dad motioned Fiona over the moment he caught sight of her.

"What's all the hubbub about?" Fiona asked.

"The reviews are in," Delia exclaimed, and read from the tablet. "It's 'a tour de force.' 'Vermont traditions with a new spin.' The bloggers are raving."

"Derek, you did it." Her dad's expression couldn't have been more pleased.

"Oh, no. We did it," he corrected, his gaze firmly fastened on Fiona. It was filled with tenderness she couldn't get enough of.

"I am so happy for the inn," Harris said. "But I'll be sad to see you leave."

His expression zeroed in on Fiona, and she knew they'd really turned a corner because the sentiment didn't make her cringe. No longer did she see the inn as a replacement for her childhood home, but an extension. Because people she cared about lived here.

They had to tell him the news.

"Don't be sad, Dad. You'll still have one of your kids around."

"Yeah. Where is he? Brandon!"

"Dad. I wasn't talking about Brandon." From the corner of her eye, she watched Brandon and Ang walk into the room together. "I was talking about me."

"What?" Her dad's gaze cut back and forth between his two kids.

Brandon grinned. "Did you tell him the news yet?"

Obviously not, the big dummy. Brandon was so besotted with Ang he couldn't even pay attention long enough to understand where they were in the conversation. "No. So Brandon's going to move into my apartment in New York. Get back into the financial game and well… I'm going to stay here for a while. Maybe a long while."

She glanced at Derek for confirmation and saw emotions in his expression that she could hardly fathom. He did want her to stick around so they could explore everything that was happening between them.

"Wait. You're staying?" Her dad's face split into a wide, slightly confused smile.

"I told Irwin no." It had taken a long time to convince Irwin this was best for her. He'd left the offer open for another twenty-four hours in case she changed her mind, but that wasn't happening.

"Really?"

She couldn't blame her father for being so slow to believe she'd changed her mind. Irwin's offer had been the stuff of dreams, both professional and financial. Very hard to turn down. Except it had been easy, given what Vermont had promised—a fresh start with Derek in a place where she could build new memories with the people she loved.

"Yeah," she confirmed.

"Oh, honey." Dad rounded the desk and swept her up in a huge hug. "It'll be great."

Well, that took care of any lingering doubt she'd had that he might not be so thrilled to lose Brandon in exchange for Fiona. Her brother had made himself a place here at the inn which would be hard to fill. She didn't even know if she should or could try. But she did know she wanted to find *her* place.

"Who knows?" she said breathlessly. "Maybe I can lure some clients up here. After all, this place worked its magic on me."

"That's fantastic." Her father hugged her again, so overcome by the news that he couldn't seem to stop.

That was okay with Fiona. They'd been at odds for so long that they had a long way to go to catch up. This new path allowed them both the latitude to do that and she couldn't be happier.

Derek stoked the fire, still necessary even this late into the spring here in Vermont. He wouldn't have it any other way. The chill outside made the inside that much cozier, especially since he had Fiona to keep him company.

They were about to start a new tradition, one he couldn't wait to share with her. He joined her where she sat in one of the comfy yellow chairs by the fireplace, sliding into the adjacent seat. "There it is. Straight from the tree…"

"To the table," Fiona said with a laugh as he placed the plate in his hand and ewer of syrup in the other on the low coffee table stretching between the two yellow chairs.

"New England bread pudding," he said. "And my—*our* maple syrup."

Tilting the ewer over the dessert, he glanced at her. Her face glowed in the firelight and she was so beautiful that he forgot everything but Fiona and this moment together. Who needed bread pudding when he had her?

The syrup still hadn't made its way out of the ewer and Fiona laughed.

"Don't hold your breath," he told her.

"It's okay. Some things are worth waiting for," she told him.

And since he had all the time in the world as they watched the slowest syrup in existence crawl toward the rim of the ewer, he pulled her into a kiss that was sweeter than anticipation and more genuine than Vermont. Finally.

EPILOGUE

The only thing better than Vermont in the late spring, when all the snow had finally melted, was Vermont in the fall. The leaves changed somewhat gradually and then *bam*. Trees transformed into torches with an explosion of orange, yellow and red at the top.

It was breathtaking.

This was the third time Fiona had gotten to see them do their magic. But it was the first time she'd experienced a Vermont fall while pregnant. And four days overdue.

"I feel like I swallowed a watermelon!" Fiona grumbled to Derek good-naturedly as she pressed on the biggest part of her enormous stomach.

It didn't ease even an iota of her discomfort, but sometimes she imagined she could feel the warmth of her baby's skin.

Derek was the most patient husband on the planet, never once growing tired of her perfectly reasonable complaints about how this baby took after him in the slow department. He or she—they didn't know the gender yet and had sworn the staff at her obstetrician's office to secrecy—should have made an appearance already and Fiona was not handling the delay well.

She wanted to meet her child. The one she'd created with Derek, the most brilliant chef in the state of Vermont and probably in the whole country. Lately, she'd eaten enough of his amazing Vermont home cooking raised to fine dining to both choke a horse and satisfy her advanced pregnancy cravings, so she considered herself an expert of the highest order.

"That's an improvement then," he teased, his eyes twinkling as he pulled her jacket from the coat closet in anticipation of the crisp fall air outside. "Yesterday, you felt like you'd swallowed a hot air balloon. I'm still trying to figure out where you would fit the basket."

"Ha, ha. If you had a kid in your stomach who punched your bladder all day long like the kangaroo kickboxing champion of the world, you wouldn't make so many jokes. I don't understand why the doctor couldn't induce me today. This is the slowest pregnancy on record."

Derek laughed and helped her with the sleeves, though how he expected her to fit into a pre-pregnancy jacket was beyond her. She barely fit in her own skin, let alone the fleece sleeves of the offending garment. But she had to put on something to brave the chill.

Brandon and Ang were getting married today.

She'd insisted that they go ahead with their original date. After all, they'd been planning this wedding for a year and had not anticipated that Derek and Fiona might accidentally conceive at exactly the wrong time. And then as her pregnancy progressed, the doctor had set a due date that seemed to work for the timing because of course she'd deliver early.

Who could have predicted that the baby wouldn't inherit Fiona's need for speed and instead, would take after his or her laid-back father? It was mind-boggling.

"You heard the doctor," Derek reminded her. "You have to wait until tomorrow to be induced because they always schedule it five days past the due date. She wants you to have a natural birth, not one that's forced, and she's giving your body that time."

Sure. Easy for the doctor to say. She wasn't the one who couldn't see her feet.

"Besides," Derek continued with his maddening logic and calm. "If you'd been induced today, you would have missed the wedding and I know you don't want that."

"No. Ang and Brandon would forgive us, but I would never forgive myself."

Derek ushered her outside where he'd pulled the truck around to the front of the Victorian style house that Fiona had stumbled over her second day on the job as a newly licensed real estate agent for the great state of Vermont. It had taken her a while to get her license since hers wouldn't transfer from New York, but it had been worth it.

Real estate in Vermont was nothing like the city but she'd learned quickly and built up a client base that had led to multiple recommendations and word of mouth. In New York, people moved frequently as they changed jobs and had more children. She'd had repeat customers on a regular basis. Not so in Vermont. People grew roots here. That's how she'd known this gorgeous pale blue house with the wraparound porch would be the perfect place to put down hers.

Hers and Derek's. They'd acted like the pregnancy had been a surprise to stave off any jokes about how they'd just gotten married a few months before, but in reality, they'd both been hoping to start their family sooner rather than later—the one time Derek had been on board with speeding things along.

Derek drove to the Inn at Swan Lake, which wasn't but a stone's throw from their home. Its location had been the deal-sealer. Derek could walk to the kitchen at the inn and of course, both were right down the street from his beloved vegetable field.

They passed by it on the right and true to form, Derek let his practiced eye rove over the rows of winter squash and pumpkins, then critically evaluated his cabbages, beets and Swiss chard. "I think those natural traps we set for the rabbits are finally working. They're avoiding the field altogether now."

They'd had a time of that problem, for sure. The wild rabbits in this area loved Derek's greens and had happily hopped and eaten their way through bushels of the stuff before they'd finally found a great solution in the no-harm traps. They had spring-loaded doors that carefully closed behind the curious rabbit who had ventured inside to snack on the beet tops Derek laced them with. Then they could release the rabbits farther down in the valley, away from his precious vegetables.

"Just in time." Fiona smoothed a hand over her belly. "I thought you were going to start sleeping in that field with a loaded shotgun after those enterprising bunnies dug under the second fence you installed."

"I'd rather hunt mushrooms," he grumbled without any real heat.

"I know how you love your mushrooms, darling."

A dozen or more cars had already crowded into the U-shaped ribbon in front of the inn. Fiona would have walked but Derek had insisted on driving "just in case" they needed to drive to the hospital. He was so cute with his contingency plans and general excitement over the baby. He'd built a cradle himself out of wood from the copse where "their" maple tree stood. That had been a sight—watching her husband chop down a tree all by himself and then patiently cutting the wood into planks he could work with.

The finished product defied all her expectations. Apparently his delicate touch extended beyond finely chopped garlic to furniture making as well. She'd commented at the time that if she'd known from the beginning that a Vermont lumberjack had so many skills, she'd have married him sooner. He'd just laughed and called it beginner's luck in a show of self-depreciation. Outside of the kitchen, he had way less of an ego, though in the kitchen, he certainly deserved to have pride in his work.

"There's a place to park." Fiona pointed to the truck-sized opening on the far side of the U, near the horse barn.

"We should have left earlier," Derek said, his father-to-be hat firmly in place. "I would have liked to be closer to the door in the event we have to make a quick getaway."

Ha. She'd said that twice this morning but he'd fussed over her and made her lie down with her feet up since she'd be on them for a couple of hours today. But now wasn't the time to remind him that they were running late due to his overprotectiveness.

"It's your own fault it's so crowded," Fiona reminded him. The inn had become something of a legend since the great blogger event of two and a half years ago. Even Ang's friends from college had all RSVPed just to get a coveted invitation to Swan Lake.

"Don't blame all of this on me. You're the one bringing more and more people from New York to Vermont with your crazy-good ability to talk dyed-in-the-wool city people into purchasing second homes in this pastoral landscape." Derek swept a hand toward the valley dotted with sprawling homesteads, many of which she had indeed sold, that spread out beyond the truck's windshield.

A pleased smile spread across her face. "Don't stop now. You're turning my head with such pretty compliments. Next you'll be telling me that I'm responsible for resolving world peace and curing the potato blight that hit upstate."

Derek rolled his beautiful blue eyes as he put the truck in Park and then helped her down from the cab, taking extra care to see that she didn't land too hard. Something got jostled anyway and that set off an annoying Braxton-Hicks contraction.

They'd bought a four-door car in anticipation of the baby coming since the truck didn't have a backseat, but starting about two weeks ago, her sweetheart husband had requested that she not drive it anywhere by herself. She'd complied happily because it meant he drove her to showings and to the obstetrician's office in the next city. Who didn't like a handsome chauffeur who smiled all the time?

They scarcely made it to the stairs before Delia bounded out of the door to engulf Fiona in a careful hug. "I keep expecting a call any minute. That is the most stubborn baby I have ever seen!"

"I know. He takes after his father," Fiona said with a side-eyed smirk at the man in question that also doubled as a way to hide a wince as her stomach squeezed in a second contraction. "And no, that is not a spoiler alert. We still don't know the gender and neither will you until we all find out together."

"Which will hopefully be tomorrow," Brandon threw in as he joined their stepmother on the porch to hug Fiona. "Not today. Hey, Fi. Wow, you're the size of a barn!"

"Thanks, and that wouldn't be such a shock if you'd visited anytime in the last couple of months," she clucked and had to laugh at herself for stealing

Delia's line as her stepmother shot her a quirky smile. It hadn't been that long ago that Delia had been reading Fiona the riot act for not making the trip to the Inn at Swan Lake more often.

She shouldn't be hard on him. Brandon had started a dotcom company that focused on personal finance about eighteen months ago and it was booming. Fiona of all people got how hard it was to balance a career, a fiancée and family in another state.

"Been busy as a beaver getting things stable so I could take two weeks off for the wedding," he said with a grin. "For some reason, Angela is totally against me working during our honeymoon, and you do not want to make a bride mad."

Derek chuckled and nodded appreciatively. "Uh, huh, I know that's right."

"If you two are done," Fiona said affectionately and smoothed back her brother's hair. "I'm so thrilled that you and Ang are finally tying the knot. Where is that gorgeous bride?"

Ang had asked Fiona to be her matron of honor, which Fiona had gladly accepted, but due to her advanced pregnancy, she hadn't been able to do as many last minute things for the bride as she would have liked. Helping her friend get ready this morning was one of them. But that didn't mean she couldn't see Ang before the ceremony.

"Right this way." Delia ushered Fiona inside and sent Derek off with Brandon to act as the best man,

221

then followed Fiona up the stairs to the top-floor suite she'd set aside for the bridal party.

The stairs shouldn't be so hard to climb! She'd done it a million times, even while pregnant. Stupid contractions. They weren't that painful. But they weren't a breeze either and the stairs didn't go well with Braxton-Hicks. She ignored them.

The entire inn had been decorated to the nth degree with fall colors of harvest gold and rich red, blooming flowers and ribbons dotting every flat surface. It was the perfect setting for a wedding, as Fiona well knew since she'd married Derek here almost a year ago.

Angela glanced behind her in the mirror as Fiona came into the room, her face lighting up. "Oh, my goodness! I know I just talked to you via videochat yesterday but you didn't tilt your phone down far enough. That baby is popping out today, I can feel it."

"I hope not." Fiona gave her friend a far too short hug. "This is your day and I am not planning to steal your thunder."

"Well, sometimes that's out of your control," Ang advised her with raised eyebrows. "As much as you'd like to say differently. I see the dress still fits."

Fiona glanced down at the off-white bridesmaid dress she and Angela had picked out together from a maternity shop online. "Barely. I've had it let out three times. You're lucky I don't float away like a big kite."

"You look beautiful," Ang insisted. "You could have worn a potato sack and that would still be true. Being in love and pregnant agrees with you."

"It does."

More than she would have ever expected. It had been tough experiencing both married life and, shortly thereafter, her first pregnancy without her friend by her side, but Ang and Brandon were building their lives together in New York. Fiona's heart was one hundred percent stuck in Vermont. Who would have guessed?

But she loved everything about this place and couldn't wait to raise her family here. Bake brownies and grill hamburgers like she'd done with her own parents, but in the home she'd created with Derek. Ang and Brandon would visit and it was enough.

"Let's get you married to my brother!" Fiona proclaimed and wrinkled her nose. "You know, assuming you like having your hair pulled. Why you want to sign up for a lifetime of *that*, I'll never know…"

Ang laughed. "These days, he's stroking my hair. So I think it's going to work out."

"It better. I'd hate to have to kill him otherwise."

The misty smile stealing over Ang's face said that wasn't likely to ever be a problem. "He's the best thing that's ever happened to me after you. How lucky am I that I get to marry Brandon Rangely *and* have you for a sister-in-law?"

"You are getting the better end of the deal," Fiona said with a laugh. "However will you repay me?"

"I'll think of something," Ang promised with a wink and stood as Delia bustled into the room followed by Ang's mother, who had the bride's veil and headpiece in her hand.

In short order, Ang was ready, glowing in her white lace dress and clutching a bouquet of winter white roses. The ladies all cried, Fiona the most—probably because of baby hormones, but she chose to believe it was due to all the happiness.

Downstairs, they took their places and the ceremony started before Fiona could catch her breath. She smiled at her father and Delia who had claimed seats in the front row and cried some more as the minister read the vows. By Brandon's side, Derek stood quietly, handsome as all get-out in his dark suit, and she couldn't tear her gaze from his face as Brandon and Ang repeated their vows.

It was a beautiful ceremony. Perfect.

Except for the part where Fiona's water broke as the minister said, "You may kiss the bride."

Brandon plunged Ang into a romantic kiss and Fiona's vision starting weaving in and out.

Oh, man. What excellent and horrible timing. Fiona pretended nothing had happened but Derek heard her audible groan as a really strong contraction tried to squeeze her in half. He rushed to her side just as piped music signaling the end of the ceremony floated through the loudspeakers in the corners of the room.

"Fiona, are you okay?" someone said. Maybe Delia.

Brandon and Ang were staring at her, as was the

entire room full of guests and all she could do was nod. "I'm afraid I'm having a baby. Like right now."

Derek didn't even hesitate, just picked her up in his strong arms and hustled her out of the inn, barely pausing at the steps. He was *carrying* her as if she weighed no more than a feather. If she hadn't already been swept off her feet, she might swoon.

"Now I know you're the man for me," she murmured as she drank in his taut, purposeful expression. "That was the fastest exit I've ever seen."

"I love you too," he said with broad smile. "Let's have a baby."

He continued his newfound love of speed by driving ninety to the hospital in the next city while instructing Fiona to breathe. Like she'd forget to or something. The contractions kept coming and by the time they got to the hospital, they were less than five minutes apart.

Fiona's obstetrician strode into the room where Fiona lay on the white hospital bed, wishing for some magic that would get this baby out. The contractions hurt and she was already tired.

"It's time," the doctor informed her cheerfully. "You ready to start pushing?"

Finally.

Hours later, the doctor placed her son in her arms. He was beautiful, just like his father. She was so tired, but this little bundle of joy had finally arrived and she didn't think she could ever put him down.

Derek, who looked like he might be a little teary

eyed, sat on the bed and stroked the little wrinkled face.

"How about if we name him Harris," Derek suggested out of the blue as if they hadn't spent the last eight months deciding on a short list of names for each gender—and Harris wasn't on it. "After your dad."

Fiona nodded, not trusting herself to speak. The name was perfect, exactly what she wanted and never realized. That was Derek's best skill—making her deliriously happy.

She hoped to spend the next fifty or so years making him just as happy. "Only if we make his middle name your father's."

The baby would have a bit of both his parents' heritage that way. Derek nodded, his eyes shining. "That's an amazing idea. Thank you."

At Fiona's insistence, Brandon and Ang attended their wedding reception and later that day, her family crowded into the hospital room. She smiled up at her father and had the distinct pleasure of watching his face as they told him they'd named the baby after him. Delia cried big happy tears as she held her grandson for the first time. Brandon and Ang stood arm in arm, grinning at everyone, subtly edging toward the door, but still in the midst of the event.

All in all, it had been a memorable day, one Fiona would never forget. But she couldn't wait to take her new family home and get started creating a lifetime of more memories. Some things were worth waiting for, but once you had them, you wanted to get started loving every second of it as soon as possible.

Fiona bent to kiss baby Harris's head at the same moment Derek did and they laughed. Her husband then kissed her forehead and snuggled in next to her in the bed, the circle of her family complete.

MAPLE GLAZED
SEA SCALLOPS

A Hallmark Original Recipe

In *Moonlight In Vermont*, Derek prepares scallops with pure maple syrup in a cooking demonstration at the MapleFaire. You don't have to be a professional chef like Derek to make this New England-inspired entrée…it's as easy as it is impressive.

Yield: 4 servings
Prep Time: 15 minutes

Cook Time: 5 minutes
Total Time: 20 minutes

INGREDIENTS

Cider Vinaigrette:
- 1½ cups apple cider
- ¼ cup cider vinegar
- 2 tbsp. shallots, minced
- 1 tsp. country Dijon mustard
- 2 tbsp. extra virgin olive oil

Maple Glazed Scallops:
- 16 large sea scallops (dry pack recommended)
- 2 tbsp. extra-virgin olive oil
- as needed, kosher salt and black pepper
- 2 tbsp. butter
- 3 tbsp. best quality maple syrup (such as Vermont maple syrup)

- 6 cups loosely packed baby greens

DIRECTIONS

1. To prepare cider vinaigrette: simmer apple cider in a small nonstick saucepan until liquid is reduced to ¼ cup. Cool.

2. Combine reduced apple cider syrup, cider vinegar, shallots, Dijon mustard and olive oil in small bowl and whisk to blend. Reserve.

3. To prepare scallops: remove the tough

abductor muscle from the side of each scallop. Dry scallops thoroughly (any moisture will cause scallops to steam rather than brown).

4. Heat a large skillet over medium-high heat for 1 minute, add olive oil and heat until oil is shimmering and starting to smoke. Season scallops with salt and pepper; gently add to hot skillet and sear undisturbed over high heat for 1½ to 2 minutes on each side, or until scallops form a golden-brown crust on each side (do not overcook). Transfer scallops to a plate.

5. Add butter and maple syrup to hot skillet and heat until butter is foaming and maple syrup is bubbly. Return scallops to skillet and heat briefly over medium-high heat to infuse flavors.

6. To serve: toss salad greens with vinaigrette; arrange on a serving platter or individual plates. Arrange scallops over greens; spoon pan sauce over scallops, if desired.

Thanks so much for reading *Moonlight In Vermont*. We hope you enjoyed it!

You might like these other books from Hallmark Publishing:

Journey Back to Christmas
Christmas in Homestead
Love You Like Christmas
A Heavenly Christmas
A Dash of Love
Love Locks

For information about our new releases and exclusive offers, sign up for our free newsletter at hallmarkchannel.com/hallmark-publishing-newsletter

You can also connect with us here:

Facebook.com/HallmarkPublishing

Twitter.com/HallmarkPublish

A Dash of Love

by Liz Isaacson

Chapter One

Nikki Turner moved around the small kitchen in the diner with ease, the space familiar and cozy. She glanced up as the bell rang again, wondering where in the world Gus was going to put all these customers. She noticed a family bustling by the diner in their winter gear, and she mourned the fact that she'd be working long past the time when the sun would set. Shame, too, when it was shining so brightly, a welcome sight after the gloomy winter they'd been having in Lakeside.

The scent of spaghetti drew her gaze from the front windows, reminding her that the orders were still piled up.

Nikki enjoyed her time in the diner, making sandwiches, slinging pie for the couples celebrating Valentine's Day a few weeks early, and ladling chili into bowls. In fact, she couldn't think of anything else she'd rather be doing.

Every seat in Gus's Kitchen had been occupied for hours, and that bell kept ringing like there was room for more. Nikki smiled as a couple who'd come in to Gus's every week for the past year greeted the restaurant's namesake and started speaking with him.

A rush of affection for the white-haired man slowed Nikki down for about two seconds. Then she put together the Kitchen's signature sandwich: pastrami and turkey with tomatoes, olives, and a special spread she'd developed over the course of six months and a lot of feedback from Gus's regulars. She grinned at the sandwich like they were old friends before setting it in the window for pickup.

She garnished her signature, secret-recipe chili with a healthy dollop of sour cream and a generous sprinkling of chopped scallions. She wanted to sneak a tortilla chip, but just because she hadn't been to culinary school didn't mean she didn't take herself seriously as a cook. She'd been working in a commercial kitchen for years, and a pro would never snack while on the job.

She put up the bowl of chili as a rousing cheer for Gus rose into the rafters. A thread of sadness pulled through her as she thought about going home tonight and not coming back to this diner where she'd worked for a year and a half. She kept the smile on her face, though, as she grabbed the next ticket from the old-school holder.

Nikki managed to chase away her worries by working as quickly as she could, getting the food out to the customers without delay, and trading quips with Angela. The waitress had become Nikki's best friend when Nikki had started at Gus's eighteen months ago, and they'd moved in together very soon after that. Angela was fun, sarcastic, and the perfect roommate for Nikki and all her quirks. And soon, they'd both be out of a job.

At least Angela had already found something else to pay the bills. Nikki, however, was having a much harder time getting something that aligned her career goals, her passion for food, and her absent degree.

Someone waved for her to come out of the kitchen, and she went to congratulate Gus while the crowd was still thick. Angela hugged him in front of the huge, multicolored *Farewell Gus!* banner, and then Nikki embraced him. He reminded her so much of her own grandfather, from the wispy white hair right down to the smell of clean and crisp dryer sheets. She wished this restaurant wasn't closing—wished she'd been able to bring it to a different ending.

But she refused to let any of her sadness show and stepped back into the kitchen. She felt most at home here, and her melancholy lifted like the steam off the huge pot of chili to her right.

By the time the restaurant closed, Nikki's pinky toe pinched in her shoes, and her back ached for a healthy dose of ibuprofen. Angela stood at the bar, putting glasses into a bin, and Nikki exhaled heavily as she sat across from her best friend.

"Has to have been our busiest day ever." She put her coat on the stool next to her and glanced over to a busboy saying his final goodbye to Gus.

Angela leaned on the counter. "It certainly was our

best tip day ever!" She tossed a napkin into the bin beside her.

"Well, get used to it, Ang. You're gonna be making a lot of tips at a place like Holly Hanson's." Though exhaustion nearly consumed her, the smile wouldn't leave Nikki's face. So this chapter was closing. She felt certain a new one would open for her the same way Ang had found a job at Holly Hanson's, the premier restaurant in the city.

Nikki had entertained the idea of applying at Holly Hanson's for about point-four seconds. But they had real chefs with tall white hats and pieces of paper testifying to their skill with a knife, spices, and flavor combinations.

"It's definitely a perk," Angela said. "But I am going to miss working with you, though."

"And I'm going to miss working." Nikki tucked her reddish-brown hair behind her ear. "I didn't get the job at Café Rouge."

Angela was kind enough to look shocked. She even sounded it when she said, "I thought they really liked you."

Nikki's smile faded. "They did, but they just don't like that I don't have a culinary degree." No one liked that, it seemed.

"That is so unfair." Her light eyes flashed with indignation. "You are, hands down, the best cook I know. And I've worked at a lot of restaurants."

Nikki shrugged and tried not to focus on the negative. She glanced around the restaurant that had become her refuge, grateful for the time she'd had here. "I sure am going to miss this place. They just don't make diners like this anymore."

Gus sidled over as Angela took her bin of dishes and trash into the kitchen, the rest of the employees finally slipping away into the night. "Not too late to take it on. I'm telling ya, someone is gonna come in and turn the place into a juice bar or something." He looked horrified at the thought, as if juice were the wrong liquid to consume at all, ever.

Sympathy settled in Nikki's heart. "Oh, Gus. You know I wish I could." And she'd never meant anything more sincerely. But working as a cook and making her own way in the city didn't leave her much money to buy a restaurant. "It certainly is a dream of mine to own a place like this one day." She watched as a waitress took the bunch of balloons floating outside the diner and walked away from Gus's. "But I don't have the money. Not to mention the lack of business experience."

"Business can be learned," Gus said in his wise voice. "But talent? That's something that just comes as a gift to you. And you, kiddo—you are talented. So you just keep your eye on the prize, and someday I'm sure you'll get your dream."

Nikki's smile returned in full force. She'd been lucky to know Gus, and she hoped she'd see him around the city after today. In fact, she made a mental note to make sure she did.

"Just don't forget to let me know when that

happens." Gus leaned forward, his face open and kind. "I may be retiring, but I'll never be too old to come and have some of your chili." He covered both of her hands with one of his. Nikki's heartstrings squeezed, and she masked her tears behind an affectionate smile.

"Speaking of chili," he said. "Will you finally tell me what your secret ingredient is?"

Nikki gave a little chuckle and tilted her head to the side. "Cinnamon candy."

"The ones I keep by the cash register for the customers?"

"Those are the ones," Nikki singsonged.

Gus chuckled and shook his head. "Well, that would explain why the jar was always empty."

As they laughed together, he switched off the last of the lights in the diner.

Nikki admired the framed menu of Gus's Kitchen she'd just picked up from the custom art shop down the street. She hung it next to the menu from King of the Court and above Alfredo & Sons.

Gus's made five framed menus, and Nikki took a moment to think about her time at each restaurant. She possessed experience in spades. Surely, someone would see that. Soon.

Sunlight streamed through the front windows of the apartment, declaring another day had begun.

Another day without a job. Another day closer to Valentine's Day. She banished the thoughts of her least favorite holiday before they could infringe on her good mood.

Angela came out of her bedroom and stalled at the sight of the bright red toaster on the table. She eyed it for a moment and then sat down. "Another toaster? Where'd you get this one?"

Nikki admired it. "Got it at the flea market yesterday. Beautiful, isn't it?" She really didn't have a lot of money to be spending on frivolous things like toasters, but she did have a lot of time on her hands. And if wandering through Lakeside and looking at antiques made her happy, why shouldn't she do it?

Angela poured herself a cup of coffee and returned to the table. "So, what's wrong with modern toasters?" She took a sip and glanced at Nikki like she already knew the answer.

Nikki shrugged, her voice much too high when she said, "Nothing. The older ones just brown more evenly."

Angela only barely refrained from rolling her eyes. "Right. You do know that our place is starting to look like a diner museum, don't you?" Her playful tone told Nikki that she didn't really care that it appeared as if a fifties diner had thrown up in their apartment.

"I'm sorry," Nikki said, a plea in her voice. "It's that I see all these things, and I just can't help but picture them in my own restaurant one day. I can't help myself." She nudged the frame a bit to the right and cocked her head to see if the menu was straight. She pushed it left again and backed away from it.

But now some of the others looked crooked. "So how was work yesterday?" She made minute adjustments to each frame.

Angela exhaled. "Tense. Going from Gus's Kitchen to Holly Hanson's is definitely a challenge. Last night, she yelled at me for carrying too many plates on my arm." She spoke with an incredulous note in her voice and took another sip from her mug.

Nikki thought for a moment. "Well, Holly Hanson's is formal dining, so I kinda see her point." Not that she'd ever been a waitress. Or eaten often in such a ritzy setting. Maybe she shouldn't have said anything.

Angela gave her a look that said she was going to let that comment pass because of their friendship. "Listen, hate to break it to you, but your favorite chef isn't the nicest chef in town." She tossed her dark brown hair over her shoulder.

Nikki abandoned the fruitless quest to ensure all the menus hung in perfectly straight lines. Disbelief tore through her. "Really?"

Angela looked a bit pained. "Really." She sighed in an I-can't-believe-I-have-to-go-back-there-tonight kind of way. "She's condescending, and she's got this diva quality about her. And to tell you the truth, you're a better chef than her."

"No, I'm a cook, not a chef." Nikki shook her head and picked up her favorite coffee mug, a tall green piece of stoneware with hand-painted red and purple flowers on it.

"Tomato, tomahto. Point is, her recipes aren't even that great."

Nikki was halfway to lifting her mug to her lips when she paused. Shock traveled through her. "Okay, I don't believe that."

She ignored Angela's little half-shrug and kept going. "I mean, she just, she came out of nowhere, and she built an entire brand. She's an award-winning chef. She's opened up an entire restaurant, and—and she's published four cookbooks in four years. It's amazing."

She didn't mean to speak so emphatically, but surely Angela didn't get it. Holly Hanson was phenomenal. They didn't just hand out awards for cooking if recipes were bad.

"Nikki, you're amazing," Angela said. "You have all the skills to achieve the same success." She watched Nikki, who simply stared at her. She and Holly Hanson weren't even in the same league. How could Angela not see that? "I'm just saying…"

Nikki appreciated the vote of confidence, deciding to take it for what it was. "Thanks, Ang." Her friend had always believed in her, and Nikki seized on to that knowledge, needing to use it as ammunition for the day's events. "Well, I'll just be happy if I can get a job." She smiled like she was thrilled to be out there, dressed like she was heading to the symphony, practically begging someone to let her cook for them. "Two more interviews to go."

"Good luck," Angela said.

Nikki picked up her mug as she stood. "Thanks."

She couldn't go to an interview—especially this first one at Finique—with only coffee in her stomach. The very idea was laughable. All women everywhere knew that a job interview, whether it was at a restaurant where a very bad breakup had happened or not, required carbs. And in Lakeside, the best place to get properly carbo-loaded was Delucci's Bakery.

Nikki entered the doors to a charming chime from the bell and approached the counter. The smell of freshly baked rolls and breads made her stomach roar. And the espresso—Nikki needed one, stat.

Trish, the owner of the bakery, was one of Nikki's favorite people on the planet. Though she probably got up in the middle of the night to come to work, she greeted everyone like they were old friends.

"Hi, good morning," Nikki said.

Trish, who was more Nikki's mother's age, beamed at her. "Good morning." Her emerald-colored sweater made her eyes seem more green than blue today. "The usual?"

"Yes, please." Nikki felt like she had someone she could confide in here in the city. Her own mother lived so far away, and she hadn't wanted Nikki to come to Lakeside in the first place. So Nikki only told her the good things about her life, reasoning that there was no sense in burdening her parents with the negative. After all, she was sure one of these two upcoming interviews would net her a job.

Trish gave her a conspiratorial look. "Double whip?"

"You know it." Nikki laughed with Trish, the weight of her interview flying away, at least for the moment.

Trish returned a minute later with a mocha latte and reached for the can of whipping cream. She squirted more than a healthy amount on top and handed the to-go cup to Nikki. "So, how's the job search going? Any luck yet?"

"No, no luck." Nikki ignored the twist in her chest. "But I'm trying to stay optimistic. I'm not gonna lie, though. It's pretty hard." She ducked her head and tucked her hair. She was wearing the right clothes today. She'd studied Finique's menu, their hours, and their history listed on their website. She knew everything about the establishment. She'd cooked at five restaurants.

"Well, I have no doubt you'll find a job soon. This is a big city with a lot of hungry people."

Nikki sipped her latte and licked the cream from her top lip. "I hope so. Because if I don't find something soon, I'm going to *be* one of those hungry people." She wanted to believe Trish with all her heart—so she did.

Trish's husband, Marty, emerged from the kitchen in the back, a tray of chocolate-drizzled biscotti in front of him. The smell made Nikki close her eyes and take a deep breath, instantly transporting her straight back to her childhood. Her grandmother had made biscotti for Christmas every year when Nikki was a little girl. Since she didn't drink, she'd taught Nikki to dip the Italian cookies in hot apple cider.

She let the memory play out as Marty set down the tray and reached for a pair of tongs. "Did I hear someone say they were hungry?" He picked up a bag.

"Ooh, fresh biscotti. You know I can't resist that." She couldn't, even if her pocketbook would take a three-dollar hit.

"My father opened these doors with this very recipe." Marty put a fresh cookie in the bag. Nikki started to pull out her wallet, a cute pink thing she'd bought for herself after her Valentine's Day fiasco two years ago.

There was that thought again. Probably because in only a few short weeks, she'd have to experience that day all over again.

Though she could stuff reminders of Valentine's Day away, she couldn't quite do the same with her memories of Finique. Her heart rate picked up, and she couldn't believe she was even considering stepping foot back inside the restaurant where her heart had been broken. But desperate times called for her to shelve her pride and hope her memories didn't suffocate her when she went to her job interview later that morning.

"No, no, put your money away," Marty said.

Nikki stared at him.

"When you get a job, then we'll let you pay," Trish said, glancing at her husband.

Their generosity touched Nikki's heart. "But—"

"You heard the missus," he said. "And trust me, you don't want to argue with her."

Trish giggled and playfully swatted his arm. "Marty."

Nikki accepted the bag with the biscotti and put her wallet away. "All right. Well, thanks." With both Trish and Marty looking at her with such affection, she inhaled. They believed in her. Angela's words from that morning replayed in Nikki's head.

She could ace this interview. She squared her shoulders and lifted her latte. "Well, I'm off to another job interview. Wish me luck!"

Read the rest! *A Dash of Love* is available now.